"Here they com

Blanca Herrera advised b
might be unaware of the pursuit.

"I see them," he replied. "Hang on."

Almost before she could react to his warning, they
cleared the alley and he cranked the Ford into the
sharpest left-hand turn he could manage, startling a
pair of jaywalkers who squealed and ran for safety
on the sidewalk. Gunfire echoed from the alley at
his back, even before the first chase car emerged.
The pedestrians went prone.

Bolan was making all the haste he dared on
residential streets, watching the sidelines where his
own headlights and those closing behind him cast
distorted, moving shadows. Any one of them might
mask another late-night rambler, possibly a child,
and Bolan had to balance that thought with the
threat of death that rode his bumper. At the same
time, if he drove too fast and lost control, smashed
up the Ford, he and his passengers were facing
sudden death, and the failure of his mission.

"Could you distract them for me?" he asked Herrera.

"How?"

"Shoot back!" the Executioner said.

MACK BOLAN ®
The Executioner

The Don Pendleton's® Executioner®

EXTREME JUSTICE

A GOLD EAGLE BOOK FROM
W★RLDWIDE®

TORONTO • NEW YORK • LONDON
AMSTERDAM • PARIS • SYDNEY • HAMBURG
STOCKHOLM • ATHENS • TOKYO • MILAN
MADRID • WARSAW • BUDAPEST • AUCKLAND

First edition August 2008

ISBN-13: 978-0-373-64357-8
ISBN-10:   0-373-64357-8

Special thanks and acknowledgment to
Michael Newton for his contribution to this work.

EXTREME JUSTICE

Printed in U.S.A.

All evils are equal when they are extreme.
—Pierre Corneille,
1606–1684
Horace

Sometimes we have to match evil with evil. It's a fact, and I'm prepared to pay the toll.
—Mack Bolan

THE
MACK BOLAN
LEGEND

Nothing less than a war could have fashioned the destiny of the man called Mack Bolan. Bolan earned the Executioner title in the jungle hell of Vietnam.

But this soldier also wore another name—Sergeant Mercy. He was so tagged because of the compassion he showed to wounded comrades-in-arms and Vietnamese civilians.

Mack Bolan's second tour of duty ended prematurely when he was given emergency leave to return home and bury his family, victims of the Mob. Then he declared a one-man war against the Mafia.

He confronted the Families head-on from coast to coast, and soon a hope of victory began to appear. But Bolan had broken society's every rule. That same society started gunning for this elusive warrior—to no avail.

So Bolan was offered amnesty to work within the system against terrorism. This time, as an employee of Uncle Sam, Bolan became Colonel John Phoenix. With a command center at Stony Man Farm in Virginia, he and his new allies—Able Team and Phoenix Force—waged relentless war on a new adversary: the KGB.

But when his one true love, April Rose, died at the hands of the Soviet terror machine, Bolan severed all ties with Establishment authority.

Now, after a lengthy lone-wolf struggle and much soul-searching, the Executioner has agreed to enter an "arm's-length" alliance with his government once more, reserving the right to pursue personal missions in his Everlasting War.

Prologue

Crooked Island, Florida
June 14

Armand Casale rose from the midnight surf, water streaming from the neoprene wet suit that covered his athletic body like a second skin. He spit out the mouthpiece of his scuba breathing apparatus and reached back with his left hand to interrupt the flow of oxygen. Leaving his face mask snug in place to spare his eyes from dripping saltwater, Casale shed his swim fins, hooked them to his belt and crossed the narrow strip of moonlit beach with long, determined strides.

He couldn't help the moon, but a mad sprint across pale sand to reach the tree line would only invite the notice of the guards.

When he reached the trees without a siren going off or shouting men rushing out to cover him with automatic weapons, Casale reckoned he was halfway home. The hardest bit was still ahead, of course, but other members of his team had worried that he wouldn't even survive the trip ashore.

Casale knew what he was doing. That was why he'd come alone, against the odds, instead of dragging half a dozen shooters with him like some kind of ragtag army launching an amphibious invasion.

Done right, it was a one-man job.

And if he failed, why take the others down with him?

His target lay a hundred yards inland. The small two-bedroom house would've sold for seven figures if it had been offered for sale. A buyer would've paid not only for the proximity to the ocean but also for the isolation, which was rare indeed wherever sand met surf around the Sunshine State.

The property was not for sale, however. Hadn't been since Uncle Sam had snapped it up during World War II for naval exercises. More recently, the Justice Department maintained the property and used it as an outpost of the WITSEC program.

Witness Security, that was.

Casale didn't know how much his boss had paid for information regarding the location of the Crooked Island safehouse, and he didn't care. He had his orders, and he meant to execute the plan without a hitch.

Four guards, at least, and one primary target. Casale was authorized to kill them all, if necessary, and to hell with any heat resulting from the deaths of federal agents.

It was perfect.

Casale wasn't sure exactly how his adversaries would be armed. The Smith & Wesson .40-caliber had been standard issue for the FBI since 1990-something. Shotguns were more than likely, though Casale couldn't rule out lightweight automatic weapons.

Never mind.

Casale was prepared for anything. In lieu of backup, he was carrying a Spectre submachine gun and accessories inside an airtight plastic bag. The weapon measured only fourteen inches with its shoulder stock retracted, twenty-two if he attached the fat suppressor to its threaded muzzle. Fifty-round four-column magazines gave the Spectre an ammo capacity surpassing any other SMG, while its cyclic rate of 850 rounds per minute bested even the classic Heckler & Koch MP-5.

The Spectre was Casale's last resort, however. He would hold it in reserve, in case the plan started to fall apart.

His two primary weapons were a customized Walther P-38 pistol, also fitted with a suppressor and hand-loaded subsonic rounds, and a brand-new toy that dangled in a scabbard on Casale's belt.

He had only used the WASP injector knife once before on a human being—call it a field test—and the results had been dramatic. The WASP carried a 12-gram cartridge of CO_2 gas inside its handle, triggered at the touch of a button through a tube in its 5.5-inch blade of razor-edged surgical steel. Upon release, forty cubic inches of gas were injected into the target's flesh at minus sixty degrees Fahrenheit, expanding to basketball size and instantly freezing soft tissue on contact.

The WASP was created as a self-defense weapon for divers confronted by sharks. Injection of the freezing gas not only killed the shark, but also caused it to rise at dangerous speed, bursting open as it reached the surface and distracting other predators while the diver escaped, forgotten.

The knife retailed for six hundred dollars, but Casale's hadn't cost him anything. One of Don Romano's thieves had stolen a case of them back in July, and Casale had appropriated two for himself, with enough gas cartridges to see him through a busy year. He had tried his new toy on a homeless man in San Francisco, two weeks earlier. Police were still puzzling over the case, while tabloid journalists beat the bushes for satanic cultists or black-market-organ harvesters.

After this night, the FBI would have a better handle on the mystery, but what of it? They might know *how*, and even *why*, but it would be a stone bitch learning *who*.

Casale slipped on the running shoes that he had carried in another plastic bag. He wasn't taking any chances with a seashell or a piece of glass that might leave blood drops for the Bureau lab rats. No one had his DNA on file so far, but why risk injury and help his enemies at the same time?

A gliding shadow in the wind-swept night, Casale slowly approached the target, taking one step at a time.

Hyder, Arizona
June 14

HAROUN AL-RACHID SUPPOSED the small town's name was meant to be a joke. Why else would agents of the U.S. government attempt to hide one of their most important turncoat witnesses in a community called *Hyder?*

It was the very sort of arrogance that most disgusted him about Americans, the smug conviction that they were superior in every way. Even their sense of humor was crude and tasteless, heavily dependent on insults directed toward nonwhite minorities or females.

Since bin Laden had surprised the Americans in 2001, Muslims had become targets of American humor. Al-Rachid understood the impulse—in truth, one of his own favorite jokes involved an American missionary and a priapic camel—but he still believed that the Great Satan needed to learn more humility.

This night, in his own small way, he was happy to help.

The desert outside Hyder, Arizona, bore no visible resemblance to that of his Saudi homeland. It lacked the massive, ever-changing dunes of perfect, almost silken, sun-baked sand. Instead, it was a place of grit and gravel, hard soil creased and creviced like an ancient reptile's skin. It sprouted cacti, Joshua trees, mesquite and tumble-weeds, those prickly, erratic travelers that still made al-Rachid's driver flinch each time once bounced across the two-lane road in front of them.

"Be careful," al-Rachid ordered. "The police are everywhere."

The driver acknowledged his order in Arabic, keeping his eyes on the highway revealed by their headlights.

In fact, except for those he'd come to kill, al-Rachid doubted that he would find another lawman in the area this evening. There was a one-man sheriff's substation in Hyder, and the district had its own highway patrolman, but al-Rachid had been assured that the sheriff's deputy went home at 6:00 p.m., except in cases of emergency, while the patrolman—called a state trooper—supervised four hundred miles of rural highway during his eight-hour shift. The odds against encountering him accidentally at any given place or time were higher than al-Rachid himself could calculate.

Upon arrival at their destination, it would be a different story. Al-Rachid and his two companions had been sent to kill one man, but he was guarded by at least four others, armed and trained.

No problem.

FBI agents—and all American police, in fact—were taught to save lives first and kill only in the utmost extremity. Nothing in their experience prepared them to match wits with dedicated warriors fielded by the Sword of Allah.

They would learn that lesson this night, to their ultimate sorrow.

Al-Rachid used a penlight to review the road map folded in his lap. He had the turnoff clearly marked, a thick black arrow pointing from the narrow highway to the right, or east.

"One mile," he told the driver. Turning toward the soldier in the backseat, he commanded, "Goggles."

Without answering, the man reached into a duffel bag on the seat beside him, drawing out two pairs of night-vision goggles. Al-Rachid took them both, placed one atop his map and held the other ready as his driver neared the access road that led to their intended target.

"Now," al-Rachid announced. The driver switched his headlights off, turned slowly off the highway to his right and stopped a few yards down the unpaved road. Brake lights glowed ruby-red behind them, but al-Rachid could not prevent it, simply offering a prayer that his enemies were less than vigilant.

He passed a pair of bulky goggles to the driver, then put on his own, adjusting the head straps until the weight was fairly balanced. Every time he wore night-vision gear for any length of time, al-Rachid wound up with aching muscles in his neck and shoulders, but it was a minor price to pay under the circumstances.

Victory was now within his grasp.

He swiveled in his seat, confirming that the backseat gunner had his goggles on, the AR-18 folding-stock assault rifle held ready in his hands. Two more identical weapons lay on the floor at al-Rachid's feet.

Given a choice, he would have picked Kalashnikovs, but in the present circumstances Armalites had been the best rifles available. They chambered 5.56 mm NATO rounds, slightly larger than the AK-74's standard 5.45 mm Soviet cartridge, but the difference in practiced hands was minimal, and the Armalite's larger 40-round magazine gave the weapons superior firepower.

Loaded with armor-piercing rounds, as these were, the rifles should defeat any Kevlar or similar protective apparel worn by the target or his bodyguards. In fact, the slugs should slice through body armor like a heated knife through cheese.

"Three-quarters of a mile," al-Rachid reminded his wheelman. The driver knew that, but reminders did no harm, and there was no objection. As they drove along the unpaved access road, raising a plume of dust concealed by midnight darkness, al-Rachid dropped his map and lifted the twin rifles from the car's floorboard.

They dared not drive directly to the house itself. Even with the headlights off, that would alert the guards and destroy their advantage of surprise. Al-Rachid would stop his driver halfway to the desert bungalow, then proceed on foot across the arid landscape to their goal.

With luck, he hoped to catch the target and at least one of his bodyguards asleep. The agents had to sleep and eat in shifts, with two or three of them remaining on alert around the clock.

But *how* alert?

Al-Rachid smiled as the car slowed, coasting to a halt.

A few more moments, and he would find out.

Crooked Island, Florida

ARMAND CASALE MET the first guard when he was still fifty yards from the house. He was surprised to find the middle-aged FBI agent at large after midnight, prowling the grounds while a chill breeze blew in from the gulf, but Casale supposed that even G-men got bored sometimes.

The agent had a riot-model shotgun, but he carried it in one hand, dangling beside his leg, its muzzle pointed toward the earth. Even if it was cocked, to fire the weapon Casale's enemy would have to shift his hold, relocate his right hand to clutch the pistol grip and let his index finger slip inside the trigger guard.

Casale didn't plan to give him time for that.

He crouched in shadow, perfectly immobile, scarcely breathing, as the roving sentry passed his hiding place. Casale saw the Kevlar vest his adversary wore, without a jacket to conceal it, and it didn't worry him.

Ironically, while varied thicknesses of Kevlar could deflect most small-arms fire, they offered no significant protection against blades.

Casale gave his target three last strides, then rose from hiding, rushed upon him from behind and clamped his left hand tight against the agent's mouth. His right hand drove the WASP's blade through the Kevlar vest, which offered no more physical resistance than a heavy overcoat.

At once, Casale triggered the release of freezing CO_2 into the G-man's body cavity. The icy gas expanded instantly, traumatically displacing heart and lungs and arresting their performance in the time it took Casale to withdraw his blade. The dead man bucked and quivered in Casale's grasp, then suddenly went limp and slumped facedown in the sand.

Casale reloaded the WASP, replacing its spent cartridge with a fresh one, then moved on. So far, his mission was on schedule, going off without a hitch.

He met no other lookouts between the killzone and the house. Approaching through the darkness, he saw lighted windows with their curtains drawn against the night, a television flickering from one room where the other lights had been extinguished.

No one saw Casale draw his silenced pistol from its plastic bag. No cameras scanned the house or yard, an oversight that would rebound against someone in Washington the next day, when the night's news broke. Armand Casale circled the safehouse clockwise, searching curtained windows for a gap that would permit a glimpse inside.

He returned to his starting point without a break.

If nothing else, the FBI was good with drapes.

Casale didn't know the walking sentry's schedule, but he guessed that thirty minutes would be stretching it. How long had the G-man been prowling when they met? It was impossible to say.

Impossible, as well, for him to guess the knocks or other recognition signals that had been arranged between the agents guarding his primary target. Locating the safehouse had been difficult enough, and costly, but his sponsor didn't have the juice to penetrate the local FBI itself and pick its brains.

No matter. Casale would make his way inside the house by any means required.

First he would try the doors.

They should be locked, of course. Locking the doors and

windows was the most basic of all security precautions. Still, even the best-trained sentries sometimes made mistakes, and if the agents in the house expected their companion to return shortly…

Casale tried the back door first, considering it the more likely choice of sentries going out to search the woods and dunes. Like many seaside homes, the safehouse's front door faced inland, while its back door and rear windows faced the sea.

Casale curled gloved fingers around the knob and tested it.

It turned.

Casale held his breath, expecting shrill alarms, a shouted warning, even gunfire.

Nothing happened.

Following the Walther's lead, he stepped into a well-lit but empty kitchen.

He crossed the room, stepped into a darker corridor that branched left and right. The television sounds came from his left, presumably one of the bedrooms. Turning to his right, he followed the drone of voices speaking quietly but with no apparent effort at concealment.

Midnight was a quiet time, and Death was near.

Casale stepped into what would've been the living room and found two agents sprawled in easy chairs, debating some fine point of the derivative team sport Americans called football. One G-man faced the doorway where Casale stood; the other had his back turned toward his assassin.

The first man lurched forward, reaching for his gun. The sudden forward motion brought his face to meet Casale's silent slug. Casale barely registered the splat of blood and brain against the chair's upholstery.

He fired again before the second man could rise and turn, his neck and torso twisted as he tried to draw his pistol, strained to glimpse his enemy.

Too late.

The second bullet drilled his temple and kept going, spilling any final thoughts across the cheap rust-colored carpet. When he fell, the impact of his body was a solid, final sound.

Two left.

Casale doubled back along the hallway, slightly worried that some noise might have alerted the safehouse survivors. He tried the first bedroom and caught the last G-man asleep, blinking defensively against the spill of light before a bullet sent him to dreamland forever.

That left one.

Casale knew his primary target wouldn't have a weapon. That was strictly, fatally forbidden by the WITSEC code. Only the guardians were armed, trusted to sacrifice themselves on the behalf of those they were assigned to watch.

Now, with the sacrifice complete, the target was defenseless.

He half expected that the last door would be locked, some vestige of a challenge for his effort, but the knob turned easily. Casale stepped across the threshold, recognized his target instantly from photos he had memorized.

The man lay on his back in bed. At the intrusion, he sat up.

"Vincent Onofre," Casale said. Not a question, simply making sure.

The target's mouth sagged open. "Who the hell are you?"

"Friend of a friend," Casale said, and shot the traitor twice. One bullet through the forehead, and another through the temple as he slumped back dead, against his stack of pillows.

Done.

It was a good night's work, with one last swim ahead of him before Casale made for home.

Hyder, Arizona

THREE MEN COULD NOT surround a house, per se, but they could cover it sufficiently by staking out three corners of the building. Each shooter thus had unobstructed views of two sides, cutting off any attempt by occupants to flee unseen.

Haroun al-Rachid claimed the northeast corner for himself, watching the north—or front—and east sides of the safehouse. Umarah, his driver, had the southeast corner, covering the east and south sides, while Tabari—on the southwest corner—watched the west and south.

Perfect.

Two lights were burning in the safehouse. One gleamed dully

through a smallish frosted pane that had to have been the bathroom window, while another shone through crooked drapes and offered sliver glimpses of the kitchen. There were no signs of movement, but al-Rachid assumed that one or two guards had to still be awake.

His plan lacked subtlety, but had the virtue of surprise and overwhelming force. He would not give his enemies a chance to fight or run. Alert or dreaming, they were bound to die.

Besides the Armalite AR-18s, al-Rachid's small arsenal included three LAW rockets, disposable bazookas featuring a lightweight plastic launching tube that held a 66 mm armor-piercing rocket with a high-explosive payload in its nose. Deemed obsolete against most modern tanks, the rockets still served well enough against civilian vehicles and homes.

As in the present case.

Al-Rachid's companions had been trained to use the LAWs, advised that they would each have one shot only and had to make it count. Thermite grenades would follow the initial blasts, and they would stay to watch the house burn to its foundation, greeting any stunned survivors with their Armalites.

Al-Rachid released his launcher's safety pin and drew it out to full length, balanced it across his shoulder as he aimed. The AR-18 rifle lay beside his right foot, in the sand, with the white-phosphorus grenade.

He armed the LAW, sighted on the window he had chosen for his target, six feet to the left of the front door, and pressed the trigger. Simultaneously, his two men released their rockets, warheads speeding toward the house with tails of fire.

Glass offered no significant resistance to the rockets. They were set to detonate on impact only with a solid wall, inside the house, where their explosive power would demolish timber, plaster, furniture and flesh.

The rockets detonated like a string of giant firecrackers, expelling smoke and shrapnel from their points of entry. Other windows of the safehouse shattered, front and back doors trembling in their frames but holding fast.

So far.

Before the echoes of the triple blast had time to fade, al-Rachid had palmed his Thermite canister, armed it, stepped closer to the stricken house and pitched it through the aperture where flames were visible already, spreading, feeding on the rubble, generating toxic smoke.

After the rockets, the grenades were relatively quiet. They made muffled whumping sounds inside the house, immediately spewing white-hot chemicals that would incinerate on contact virtually any man-made substance. Thermite would burn through tempered steel and concrete. Flesh and bone were nothing, in the scheme of things.

Al-Rachid stood waiting with his Armalite in hand, watching the safehouse burn. He felt the heat from where he stood and knew it had to be hell in there, almost beyond imagining. Still, traitors who abandoned sacred oaths of loyalty deserved no less. The Thermite blaze would give his target a foretaste of hell.

Justice.

Another job well done.

Al-Rachid was starting to relax when bullets churned the sandy soil around his feet, making him skip and dance away. He found cover behind a nearby Joshua tree, amazed that anyone was still alive inside the house, much less in any shape to fight.

Al-Rachid first told himself it might be ammunition cooking off inside the fire, but it defied the laws of physics that a clutch of random cartridges exploding could produce the pattern that had nearly cut his legs from under him.

Those shots were aimed by someone who had managed to survive both rockets and grenades.

So be it. They had planned for this.

Al-Rachid waited, resisted the impulse to fire back at the winking muzzle-flash he glimpsed sporadically. The raging fire would either eat his enemy alive or drive the man from cover where he could be shot at leisure.

All Haroun al-Rachid had to do was watch and wait.

Five minutes later, just when he'd begun to listen for the wail of sirens in the distance, al-Rachid saw a shadow figure move against the background of the flames. It lurched and staggered, nearly doubled over as the sole survivor of the holocaust hacked smoke and other fumes out of his lungs. Al-Rachid could not identify the weapon in his adversary's hands and didn't care to try.

He fired a long burst from the Armalite, expending half a magazine when two or three rounds would have sufficed. Al-Rachid was angry at his target, recognized the feeling as irrational and still allowed himself the luxury of overkill. His bullets dropped the man, then set his corpse to twitching, jerking on the arid soil.

When it was truly finished, when the safehouse had collapsed into itself and every part of it was totally engulfed by fire, al-Rachid beckoned his soldiers and they walked back toward their waiting vehicle.

1

Mack Bolan held the rented Ford at a nerve-racking fifty miles per hour, staying with the flow of traffic that jammed Avenida Central without ever seeming to slow its pace or stop for red lights. He kept a sharp eye on the drivers around him, many of them seemingly intent on suicide, while flicking hasty glances toward his rearview mirror, watching for police cars.

Bolan didn't even want to think about what local law enforcement might say about a gringo driving through their capital with military hardware piled up in the backseat of his rental car.

"How much farther?" Bolan asked his navigator.

Blanca Herrera was a thirty-something knockout, her angel face framed by a fall of glossy jet-black hair, above a body that could grace a calendar.

Herrera checked the city street map, measuring with slender fingers. "Two kilometers, perhaps," she said at last. "Turn right on Calle Quarenta—or Fortieth Street, you would say—then drive north to Avenida Cinco."

"Right."

Fifth Avenue. Unfortunately, they weren't going to a fashion show at Sachs.

"If I may say again—"

He cut her off. "No calls. No warnings."

"But I wouldn't have to speak."

"Hang-ups are worse. We can't do anything to spook him now."

The lazy shrug did interesting things inside her clinging blouse. "Ah, you know best. But if he is not home when we arrive…"

"We wait," he finished for her. "Find a vantage point and settle in."

"However long it takes?"

"Unless you know some way to read his mind and tell me where he's gone."

"No," Herrera replied. "I can't do that."

"Well, then."

"This gringo is *muy importante,* yes?"

"*Muy importante,* right."

"But you expect to find him home alone? No bodyguards?"

"Gil Favor likes his privacy," Bolan replied. "Besides, he's paid your government for years to keep him safe and sound."

"Some individuals, perhaps," she answered somewhat stiffly.

"The police, the prosecutors and at least one president."

"*Ex*-president," the sultry woman corrected him.

"Whose squeaky-clean successor hasn't made a move to change the status quo where Favor is concerned."

"Are you forgetting that we have no extradition treaty with your country?"

"Nope. Neither is good old Gil. That's why he didn't need a troop of heavies. Until now."

"And you believe he will be unaware of any recent danger to himself?"

"I've got my fingers crossed," Bolan replied.

That was the rub, of course. The FBI and U.S. Marshals Service had been sitting on the WITSEC murders, pulling every string available to maintain a media blackout, but any form of censorship had limits and the voluntary kind was typically as leaky as a sieve. Even without the press or television, Favor would have contacts in the States to warn him of a shift in climate, someone turning up the heat.

What would he do? Sit tight or run for cover with a new identity established in advance? Was he already running, gone before Bolan could corner him?

Or had the others, those who wanted Favor dead, already come and gone?

We'll see, Bolan thought. It wouldn't be much longer now.

"I've been here once before," he said. "But farther south."

"A job like this one?"

"Not exactly."

"I am sorry," Herrera informed him, face diverted to scan shops and restaurants. "It's not my place to ask such things."

"You're right."

She knew better, but they'd run out of small talk after ten or fifteen minutes. "If we find Favor at home—"

"We'll find him."

"*When* we find him, what approach will you be using?"

"Short and not so sweet," said Bolan. "Someone wants him dead. His best chance of survival is to hop a flight with me and put his enemies where they can't do him any harm."

"Will he believe that? Knowing who and what they are?"

"No way."

Gil Favor wasn't stupid. He was something of a genius, in fact, where numbers were concerned, and he was also as crooked as a swastika. He'd realize that locking up the man in charge, even inside a death row cage, wouldn't remove the price tag from his own head. Whether Favor testified or not, his chances of survival on the street—or anywhere outside protective custody—were slim to none.

"Why should he help you, then?"

"It's my job to persuade him," Bolan answered.

"And may I ask how you intend to do that?"

Bolan frowned, making his right-hand turn, dodging a motorcyclist who seemed to think lane markers were an optical illusion. His answer was curt and to the point.

"I'll let him flip a coin."

"I'm sorry?"

"Give the man a choice," Bolan elaborated. "He can deal with me right now, or with someone else's shooters down the line."

"I see. And if he's not persuaded by your logic?"

"Favor's coming with me one way or another," Bolan said. "This time next week, he'll be in New York City, on a witness stand."

"What happens if you take him all that way and he refuses to cooperate in court?"

"Somebody else's problem," Bolan answered. "My job is finished on delivery."

They rode in silence for a time, then Bolan saw the sign and said, "Fifth Avenue."

"Go west," Herrera said. "His house will be the third one on our left."

Bolan followed her directions, thankful that the major rush of traffic was behind them. Fifth Avenue was quiet by comparison, with stately homes on either side.

Here's money, Bolan thought as he counted houses on the left.

"You see it, yes?" she asked. "Just there, the brick and stone."

"I see it," Bolan said. "And he's got company."

GIL FAVOR DIDN'T SIMPLY *like* his privacy. He craved it, needed to be left alone the same way that he needed food, water and oxygen. It was the best—perhaps the only—way for him to stay alive.

Throughout his forty-seven years, no single interaction with the other members of his species had left Favor with a sense of what his fellow humans called fulfillment. Granted, he was happy while stealing and spending someone else's hard-earned money, even found release with prostitutes who idolized him for an hour with the meter running.

But as far as anything resembling a normal life?

Not even close.

That was to be expected now, given the circumstances of his present situation. He had millions of dollars in a bank account the U.S. government could never crack, lived well beyond the reach of federal warrants and didn't really mind being a man without a country in his middle age.

He was about to pour himself another after-dinner brandy when the first alarm chimed softly. Nothing to get overwrought about, beyond the fact that any chime at all meant trespassers outside his home.

Now what the hell?

Favor had never been a violent man—well, almost never. He had earned the bulk of his ill-gotten gains by cooking the books and washing blood money for heavy-duty predators, skimming off a portion for himself when the distractions of a thug's life blinded him to what was happening beneath his very nose.

Still, the survival reflex was as strong within Gil Favor as in any other human being who had lived by wits and guile for the majority of his or her life.

A second, louder chime told Favor that his uninvited guests were drawing closer to the house, along the driveway from the street outside. He wasn't expecting any deliveries, but his mind still offered innocent suggestions for the visit.

Fat chance, however.

In four years and counting in his minipalace, he'd never had a salesman on his doorstep. No neighbors visited without an invitation, and he hadn't issued any.

That meant trouble was coming, one way or another.

Favor set down his brandy snifter, rose from his recliner and retrieved the sawed-off shotgun from its hidden cubbyhole beside the liquor cabinet. The first cartridge was rock salt, for a wake-up call; the four that followed it were triple-aught buckshot.

"You should've picked another house," Gil Favor muttered as he left his study, moving briskly toward the parlor and front door.

THE OCCUPANTS OF TWO CARS were unloading near the mansion's broad front porch as Bolan passed the driveway, counting heads. He saw no uniforms, no proper suits that would've indicated plain-clothes officers.

"They're not police," he said.

"What, then?" Blanca Herrera asked. "Maybe he has a dinner party."

"Doubtful," Bolan said. "You saw them, right? They don't fit with the neighborhood."

"He is a fugitive from justice," she reminded him. "Why would his friends be chosen from the social register?"

"Good point."

But Bolan knew Gil Favor wasn't one for making friends. And if he *did,* the self-made billionaire would handpick those who best served his camouflage of affluent respectability.

"Why are you stopping?"

"I just want to check this out," Bolan explained. "If they're sitting down to surf and turf, we'll wait and tag him after they go home."

"And if it's something else?" Herrera asked. "What then?"

He nosed the Ford into an alley two doors down from Favor's driveway, switching off the lights and engine. "Then I intervene," he said.

"Against eight men?"

"I'll do my best."

She scrambled out to join him in the darkness, while he was extracting hardware from the larger of two duffel bags on the backseat.

"You can't be serious!"

"I've left the keys," he told her. "If it gets too raucous, or I'm not back here in fifteen minutes tops, clear out."

Herrera gnawed her lower lip, then said, "I'm coming with you."

"No, you're not."

"How will you stop me?"

He pinned her with a glare that made her take a slow step backward. "This is my part of the deal," he said. "You got me here. Now step aside and let me work."

"I'm fully trained," she challenged.

"Not for this."

"How would you know?"

He fought an urge to squeeze her slender neck just hard enough to break her grip on consciousness for twenty minutes, give or take. But what might happen if he left her in the car that way?

"All right," he said through gritted teeth. "You asked for it."

Her smile was fleeting but triumphant. Bolan wondered if she would live to regret her rash choice.

Already armed with a Beretta Model 92, snug in its armpit rig, Bolan retrieved a classic Uzi submachine gun from his duffel bag of lethal gear, spent three seconds attaching a suppressor to its threaded muzzle, filled his pockets with spare magazines to feed the SMG and clipped a flash-bang grenade to his belt.

His overanxious sidekick wore some kind of smallish pistol tucked inside her waistband. From his quick glimpse of its grip and the extended magazine, Bolan surmised either an HK4 or Walther PPK. She didn't ask for anything more powerful as he prepared to leave the car, and Bolan hoped that she would have the sense to simply stay out of harm's way.

Assuming that was possible.

They walked back from the alley to Favor's driveway, Bolan covering the Uzi with his windbreaker. No traffic passed them on the quiet street, but he imagined neighbors peering from their windows, wondering about the sudden flurry of activity at Señor Favor's place.

They wouldn't call for the police right now, but at the sound of gunfire...

Bolan scanned the sweeping driveway and the house beyond, saw no one standing near the cars that had pulled in a moment earlier. Eight men had either gone inside the house or fanned out to surround it, vanishing from Bolan's field of view.

"What now?" Herrera asked. "Do we knock on Favor's door?"

"Not quite," he said. Spotting the motion sensors ranged along the driveway, Bolan added, "Follow me. Stay off the pavement."

She followed without asking questions. Bolan took advantage of the property's strategically located trees as he approached the mansion, moving at an urgent pace. He had discounted booby traps upon discovering that Favor had no gate to keep stray dogs or children from the occacional intrusion. Blowing them to smithereens or crushing tiny ankles in a leghold trap would certainly have caused his stock to plummet with the neighbors.

"Don't you think—"

He shushed her with a hiss and kept moving toward the house. They'd closed the gap to twenty yards or so when muffled gunfire echoed from inside the house. A shotgun, by the sound of it, one blast immediately followed by the pop-pop-pop of pistol fire.

Bolan made for the front door, thinking it would be the quickest way to get inside the house. He didn't care if it was locked, already thinking past the first obstruction, wondering if he had come too late and Favor was already dead.

Vengeance was one thing he could definitely handle, but it would mean mission failure and freedom for another predator three thousand miles away.

He reached the porch and found the front door levered open, then pushed shut again by someone who had come before him. Bolan shouldered through it, smelling gunsmoke as he crossed the threshold.

LUIS RODRIGUEZ CLUTCHED his Ingram MAC-10 SMG and waited for a target to present itself. Nearby, not quite within arm's reach, his point man lay facedown on white shag carpeting.

The gringo had surprised them with a shotgun blast from nowhere that had toppled Paco Obregon before they even glimpsed the man they'd come to kill. It was supposed to be an easy job, and now Rodriguez thought maybe he wasn't being paid enough.

Their target was holed up inside a room no more than twenty feet from where Rodriguez crouched behind a sofa, painfully aware that springs and stuffing would not save him if the gringo kept on shooting. A glimpse had shown Rodriguez books inside the room, perhaps some kind of library. They'd have to rush the gringo soon, behind a wall of lead, and—

What was this?

Madre de díos!

Right before his eyes, Obregon was struggling to his feet, gasping and coughing, one hand pressed against his stomach while the other fumbled for his pistol on the carpet.

White shag carpet, without any stain of blood.

Rodriguez watched as Obregon brushed the rock-salt pellets from his shirt, wincing at contact with the bruised flesh underneath.

It was a trick! The damned gringo had tried to scare them off, as if Rodriguez and his men were children. The warning shot would cost the gringo his life.

Rodriguez was about to order the attack, when Paco Obregon retrieved his pistol, snarled a curse and rushed the door alone. A second, louder shotgun blast rang out, and this time there was blood aplenty, spilling everywhere as Paco vaulted over backward, crumpling in an awkward attitude of death.

Rodriguez crouched lower behind the sofa, all thoughts of

rushing the door banished from his mind. Yet he couldn't simply wait there and allow the gringo to terrorize him into immobility.

He had six more handpicked killers left, against one man who was accustomed to the soft life, swaddled by his money. Not so soft that he'd forgotten how to pull a trigger, obviously, but it would be shameful to retreat.

Worse yet, it would be fatal.

If Rodriguez failed, it wouldn't be enough to simply return the money. He couldn't just apologize and take a scolding.

No.

The man who had employed him wanted blood.

Rodriguez flashed hand signals at the two men he could see. The other four had entered through the back door of the mansion and were doubtless waiting for his signal somewhere on the far side of the library.

Frontal assault was the only option that he could think of, and if that meant losing men, so be it. He would be behind them all the way.

Rodriguez flashed another hand sign, and his soldiers nodded in response, both edging forward, clutching weapons tightly. They didn't look at Obregon, leaking blood on the carpet, but rather focused on their target. Like professionals.

Rodriguez nodded, and they rose together, shoulders hunched into the charge—then started jerking, twisting, lurching through the half steps of some crazy, spastic dance Rodriguez didn't recognize. It took a heartbeat for his mind to grasp what he was seeing, then he heard the whisper-stutter of an automatic weapon with a silencer attached.

His soldiers fell together, nearly sprawling over Obregon's limp corpse. Rodriguez spun to face the new and unexpected source of peril, squeezing off a burst with his Ingram before he had a target in his sights.

Diving and rolling, wishing that the parlor's furniture were made from steel and concrete rather than mere wood and fabric, Rodriguez glimpsed another gringo firing at him with some kind of submachine gun.

Bullets ripped through the upholstery of the stout recliner where he'd come to rest. Rodriguez raised his hand into the gringo's line of fire, emptied the Ingram's magazine and hastened to reload.

The target was supposed to be *alone,* goddamn it! He'd been told that there would be no bodyguards. It was a promise. In and out, with nothing to detain him at his task.

Bastards! Rodriguez vowed that if he made it out of this alive, there would be hell to pay.

Near panic, sweating through his rumpled shirt despite the mansion's air-conditioning, Rodriguez started barking orders to the four surviving members of his crew. He didn't know if either of his gringo enemies spoke Spanish, and he didn't care. It was still five men against two, and Rodriguez could live with those odds.

One of the other soldiers answered him, a grim affirmative. It was enough.

Rodriguez broke from cover, bellowing his rage and firing from the hip with his MAC-10.

A BURST FROM BOLAN'S muffled Uzi dropped the shouting gunman in his tracks. That made four down, and he could hear the other four men of the home-invasion team before he saw them, coming down the hall in a stampede, all firing on the run.

Bolan saw nothing to be gained by waiting until they were visible. The hallway was a killing pen. He held down the Uzi's trigger, sweeping its muzzle back and forth, vaguely aware of bright spent brass cascading from the SMG's ejection port.

An instant later, Bolan's targets stumbled into view, three of the four still firing, but without a focus to their aim. They peppered walls, floor and ceiling as their feet got tangled up and brought them crashing down. Except for all the blood and screaming, it resembled something from a slapstick comedy.

Bolan reloaded, watched the dying shooters long enough to satisfy himself that none of them presented any threat. Gil Favor hadn't joined the turkey shoot, apparently preferring to remain invisible and bide his time. Bolan edged forward now, conscious of his female companion moving on his flank, her pistol leveled in a fair two-handed grip.

"Favor!" Bolan called out. "We need to talk."

"So talk," a strained voice answered. "I've already called for the police. Let's chat until they get here, shall we?"

"That's a bad idea," Bolan replied.

"For you, maybe."

"I didn't come to hurt you," Bolan told him.

"Right. I guess you're with the neighborhood welcoming committee, then."

"I'm not with *these guys*. If I was, why would I kill them for you?"

"I don't give a shit. If you think I'm walking out of here before this place is full of uniforms, you need to have your head examined."

"The police can't help you now," Bolan stated.

"I'll just take your word for that, shall I?"

"I'd recommend it."

"Sure you would. Why don't I shoot myself right now? Spare you the trouble."

"I was sent to bring you out of here alive."

"To where?" Favor demanded.

Bolan took a chance. "Back to the States."

The hidden fugitive barked laughter. "Thanks but no thanks. I don't fancy serving thirty years."

Bolan glanced at his watch, frowning. How long until the sirens wailed outside?

"I'd say you're in a no-win situation, staying here," Bolan replied. "The cops you bought and paid for won't be watching when the next hit team shows up to finish this."

"Who says I'll be here?" Favor challenged.

"They'll be waiting for you by the time the uniforms clear out tonight, if they're not here already."

"Pull the other one, my friend. I'm sitting tight."

I don't think so, Bolan thought, but he said, "Your call."

"Damned right it is!"

Bolan unclipped the stun grenade and pulled its pin, ignoring Herrera as he moved in closer to the door that stood ajar, concealing Favor from his view. He'd have six seconds from the time he made the pitch, before his canister lit up the library.

"Hey!" Favor called out from the shadows. "You still there?"

I'm here.

The toss was easy, with a rebound from the doorjamb, putting it across the threshold. Favor blurted out a curse and started scrambling, but he had nowhere to go. Bolan dropped to a crouch, closing his eyes and clapping hands over his ears, hoping the lady would be smart enough to do likewise.

The blast was blinding, stunning, but not lethal. Bolan pushed into the smoky library and found Gil Favor writhing on the floor, convulsed and semiconscious. Once he'd kicked the shotgun out of reach, Bolan reached down and hoisted Favor to his feet, stood underneath the fugitive's left arm—and found Herrera on his other side, gripping the right.

"We're out of time," he said. "Let's go."

She flashed a smile and said, "I've been waiting for you."

They half dragged Favor from the house, past corpses, out the front door and across the sloping lawn. Bolan could hear sirens in the distance as they reached the sidewalk.

Favor was stumbling, not quite helping, by the time they reached the rental car. Bolan stashed the duffel bags of weapons in the trunk, then shoved Favor into the backseat.

"You stay with him," he commanded. "Keep him quiet."

It was a relief to get no argument.

He slid into the driver's seat, turned the ignition key and winced as sudden headlights made it high-noon bright from one end of the alley to the other.

In the rearview, Bolan saw no flashing colored lights atop the car behind him. Maybe not police, then. But—

The muzzle-flashes settled it.

He had been bluffing Favor on the backup murder team, but it was true, and they had found him.

Bolan slammed the rental car into gear and stood on the accelerator, tires smoking as he fishtailed from a standing start.

2

Near Stony Man Farm, Virginia
Monday, June 18

The helicopter pilot held his altitude near treetop level as he took the chopper southwest, following the track of Skyline Drive along the stark spine of the Blue Ridge Mountains. The Hughes 500 chopper cruised at 137 miles per hour, making it a relatively short trip for the passenger who'd boarded in Washington, D.C.

Mack Bolan didn't mind the lack of opportunity for leisurely sightseeing. He had made this trip before, with variations, covering the same ground time and time again. Once, he had fought and bled for some of it, but that was ancient history.

This day was business. He was not a tourist, didn't need to get his money's worth from every mile.

"Five minutes, sir," the pilot said, alerting him.

Bolan made no reply, waiting to catch his first glimpse of Stony Man Farm.

It was a working farm, which meant that crops were sown and cultivated, harvested and sold.

The "farmhands" who performed the daily chores at Stony Man were soldiers—Special Forces, Army Rangers, Navy SEALs, Marine Reconnaissance—all sworn to secrecy regarding their assignments at the Farm. They knew it was some kind of sensitive facility, and nothing more.

The helicopter pilot started speaking rapidly into his microphone, exchanging codes, responding to inquiries, satisfying Stony Man security that he and his lone passenger were who and what they claimed to be.

Failure of that test would produce immediate, dramatic, frightening results. The Farm's AH-1 Huey Cobra attack helicopter stood ready to deal with intruders on two minutes' notice. The Farm's defense system also included Stinger shoulder-launched surface-to-air missiles and strategically located .50-caliber Gatling guns with a maximum cyclic fire rate of 2,000 rounds per minute. And that was a fraction of the armory.

Long story short, no aircraft of any description landed at Stony Man Farm without clearance.

Bolan's chopper approached the helipad, fifty yards from the plain-looking farmhouse and equidistant from the nearest outbuilding. No casual observer would've guessed at what went on inside the nondescript buildings. Even the radio aerials and satellite dishes were cleverly concealed.

As they were touching down, Bolan saw Hal Brognola coming out to meet him. Barbara Price walked beside the man from Justice, on his left. Other Stony Man personnel would be hard at work inside on one thing or another. Bolan's afternoon arrival wouldn't cause the long-term regulars to miss a beat.

They dealt with life-or-death decisions every day.

"Something important," Brognola had told him on the scrambled sat phone. "We can talk about it when you get here."

Brognola's summons wasn't that unusual, although they sometimes met at other sites. A visit to the Farm didn't suggest the matter on the table was more critical or dangerous than one they might discuss by telephone. It might, however, mean that Brognola required the Farm's sophisticated AV gear to make his presentation.

The chopper settled and his pilot killed the engine, waiting for the twenty-six-foot rotor blades to slow, their tips drooping. Bolan unbuckled, thanked his pilot for the lift and disembarked.

"Glad you could make it," Brognola said, pumping Bolan's hand.

"No problem," Bolan answered.

Price's handshake was professional, the final squeeze a bonus, like her smile.

"I've got lunch and a presentation set up in the War Room," Brognola explained. "We'll head on down, unless you need to freshen up."

"I'm good," Bolan assured him.

"Good," the big Fed echoed. "Good is good."

Bolan found Aaron "The Bear" Kurtzman waiting to greet him in the soundproofed, air-conditioned War Room.

Bolan met the Farm's technical wizard halfway to the conference table, stooping slightly for their handshake since Kurtzman was in his wheelchair. Paralyzed by bullet fragments in his spine the day a band of renegade commandos raided Stony Man, Kurtzman had left intensive care with grim determination to never let the shooting slow him down.

Those who were standing settled into chairs, Brognola at the table's head, Bolan and Price flanking him. Kurtzman took his traditional position at the AV console.

"Right," Brognola said. "Let's get this party started."

The big Fed cleared his throat and waited for the first slide to appear onscreen behind him.

Half-turned to face the screen, Brognola saw a full-face mug shot of a swarthy man, black hair combed back from an aristocratic forehead, eyes nearly as dark pointed like twin gun barrels toward the camera. The face, though full, tapered to a decisive chin. Its mouth seemed nearly lipless, like a razor slash. The nose had once been broken, then reset with fairly decent skill. Less care had been applied to mend an older wound beside the left eye, pale scar tissue trailing onto the cheek.

"Antonio Romano," Brognola announced, "described by certain tabloid writers in New York as 'the last Don.'"

"I wish," Bolan replied.

"Romano heads what used to be the Marinello Family. You remember Augie, I suppose?" Brognola asked the Executioner.

Bolan nodded. "I had to kill him twice."

"Romano's not that durable, but he's been lucky," Brognola continued. "Until two months ago, that is. A federal grand jury in Manhattan slapped him with a couple dozen racketeering charges, this and that, then hit him with the clincher—two counts of conspiracy to aid a terrorist attack on the U.S., collaborating with the Sword of Allah."

"That's a new one," Bolan said.

"Damned right. If he goes down for that, he's gone for good. Maybe the needle, if the prosecution proves his link with a September bombing near the UN building."

"How's it look?" Bolan asked.

"It was looking great," the big Fed said, "until last Thursday night."

"What happened?"

"Basically, the roof fell in."

Brognola nodded for another slide. Romano's frowning visage was replaced with two faces side by side. The face on the left had a weasely look, long and lean, while the other was softer, more cultured. The weasel had long, greasy hair. His companion was going bald and wore a pair of gold-rimmed trifocals.

"These are—*or were*—the prosecution's two key witnesses. The rodent on the left is Emmanuel Agostino, aka 'Manny The Ferret.' Go figure. He was a capo in Romano's Family, working the waterfront. DEA caught him moving a heroin shipment from Turkey without Don Romano's approval or knowledge. That puts him *underneath* the doghouse, whether he's convicted or acquitted. Stealing from the Family and risking a conspiracy indictment on the *Racketeer Influenced and Corrupt Organizations Act,* Manny was smart enough to know he had no future if he didn't cut a very special deal."

"Which was?" Bolan asked.

"Manny's waterfront connections were diverse," Brognola said. "One of them was a Saudi sporting diplomatic papers—and immunity—who acted as liaison with a Sword of Allah sleeper cell in Brooklyn. They were buying stolen weapons, ammunition and explosives from Romano's people, getting ready for a killer party set to go on New Year's Eve."

"This wasn't on the tube," Bolan observed.

"It got the silent treatment," Brognola explained. "Homeland Security assumed correctly that they'd only clipped a weed but hadn't found the roots. Meanwhile, Manny was talking up a storm. He finally directed G-men to the fellow on your right."

"Who is…?"

"Dr. David Tabor, born Dawud Tabari in San Diego, with a Syrian father and an Irish-American mother. Tabari changed his name legally to Tabor at age nineteen, after his parents went down in a murder-suicide. According to police reports, Dad talked himself into believing Mom was stepping out and satisfied his 'honor,' then remorse kicked in. One instant orphan in his freshman year at Stanford premed. Dad's insurance wouldn't pay off for a suicide, but Mom's had a double-indemnity clause for accidental death."

"Murder's an accident?" Barbara Price asked.

"It is, in life-insurance-speak," Brognola said, "unless the beneficiary took out a contract on the dear departed. As it was, the father wouldn't have received a dime, but since he shot himself, Tabor banked a tax-free million bucks that carried him through med school and beyond."

"I'm not seeing the terrorist connection," Bolan said.

"Something the kid picked up from Daddy," Brognola replied. "Namely, hatred of Israel, Jews and anyone associated with them—which includes the U.S. government. He kept a low profile during med school, his internship and residency, then he put out feelers to the dark side and hit pay dirt. For the past five years, at least, he's been performing services for members of the Sword, Hamas and other radical Islamic groups here in the States."

"What kind of services?" Bolan asked.

"Medical. He's like one of the old mob doctors from the thirties, but he's not a quack and never lost his license. Any terrorist who's injured in the line of duty, Tabor is on call to patch them up without reporting it to the authorities. And did I mention he's a plastic surgeon?"

"Ah."

"You see the possibilities," Brognola said.

A nod from Bolan, no response required.

"Long story short, Manny The Ferret got a line on Tabor somehow, dealing with the other side, and when he rolled he took the sawbones with him. Gave him up first thing, and then the *doctor* rolled." Brognola shrugged. "I guess they don't make zealots like they used to."

"Seriously," Price said.

"Between the two of them, they linked Romano to the Sword of Allah, and Romano was indicted on a list of charges that were meant to keep him out of circulation till the next millennium, whether or not he made it to death row. His trial is scheduled to begin three weeks from Tuesday. That's tomorrow, by the way."

"About that falling roof," Bolan reminded him.

"I'm getting there. Manny and Dr. Tabor both went into WITSEC, pending their appearance at the trial. The Bureau had them separated, Manny on an island off Florida's gulf coast, the doctor out in small-town Arizona. Thursday night, a couple hit teams dropped them both, with all their guards. We lost the witnesses and eight G-men. Guess I don't need to tell you the attorney general's pissed."

"I hear you," Bolan said. "But what can I do?"

"Well," Brognola said, "as luck would have it, there's still one more witness who could make the case."

Bolan could see where the man from Janice was headed. "Who is it?" he asked.

Brognola nodded, Kurtzman keyed another slide, and Bolan watched a new face surface as the dead men faded. This man was clearly accustomed to the soft life, with an oily shine to his wavy hair and a neatly trimmed mustache. The eyes were gray-green, curious. Beneath the cookie duster, pink lips formed a careless smile.

"That's not a mug shot," Bolan said.

"He's never been arrested," Brognola replied, "but it was close. The name may be familiar. Gilbert Favor?"

"What, the Wall Street guy?"

"None other," Brognola confirmed. "They called him Vesco Junior when he split, going on eighteen months ago. The SEC brought charges on a string of junk-bond scams that made Favor a billionaire. And yes, that's with a *b*. Clearly, he wasn't stupid. Someone he'd been paying for insurance tipped him off the night before his charges were announced, and Favor caught the red-eye down to Mexico, then on from there to Costa Rica, where we haven't got an extradition treaty. He can live a sultan's life down there until he's older than Methuselah, and we can't touch him."

"Legally," Bolan amended.

"Right."

"What ties him to Romano?" Bolan asked.

"Junk bonds weren't Favor's only pastime," Brognola responded. "He's a money mover, good with numbers in the *Rain Man* kind of way. What it looks like now, he laundered cash for half the East Coast Mobs before he hit a little snag on Wall Street and got burned. One of his clients—based on testimony from the late, unlamented Ferret—was Antonio Romano. Favor did some banking for the former Marinello Family, saw where the money came from, where it went. The whole nine yards, in short."

"And he can tie Romano to the Sword of Allah?"

"Manny says—*said*—that he can. The problem, as you see, is twofold."

"How to bring him back, and how to make him talk," Bolan said.

"We'll take care of Part B," Brognola assured him. "All you need to do is drop in, have a chat with Favor and convince him to perform his civic duty."

"Just like that."

"I may have understated its complexity," Brognola granted.

"Uh-huh."

"But seriously," Brognola pressed, "we think it's doable. We've got someone on the ground to help you out. Translator, guide, chief cook and bottle washer."

"It's Costa Rica," Bolan said. "We have to take for granted that he's greased the law and politicians."

Brognola nodded. "Oh, big-time, I wouldn't be surprised."

"No reason I can think of why he ought to come back voluntarily."

"Nothing occurred to me," the man from Justice said.

"So, it's a kidnapping on hostile turf."

"These days, we call that a rendition," Brognola corrected.

"Call it anything you like. It could get messy."

"Diplomatically, of course, we can't appear to be involved."

Meaning I'm on my own, as usual, Bolan thought.

"Who else knows about Favor?"

"Well," Brognola said, "Romano, obviously."

"Does Romano know you're looking for him?"

"Hard to say. We have as many leaks in Washington and New York as we ever did. For sure, Romano knows the state's primary witnesses are dead. And since the charges haven't been dismissed, he knows the prosecution plans to go ahead with something else."

"So it's a race," Bolan said. "And I'm starting out behind the pack."

"I grant you, it's a challenge," Brognola said.

Or a death sentence, Bolan thought.

But he said, "I'll need his file."

San José International Airport
June 18

THE WORST THING about red-eye flights was arriving at some ungodly hour in a deserted airport terminal. The shops and restaurants were closed, shuttered and dark. No throng of passengers or loved ones armed with flowers and balloons greeted arriving flights. Footsteps rang hollowly on concrete floors, while dull-eyed custodians pushed their brooms along the concourse.

Granted, 9/11 and the war on terror had imposed some barriers to any overt ambush in an airport, but the dead zone of a terminal at 2:00 a.m. reminded Bolan of occasions in the old days, when he'd left commercial flights to find guns waiting for him in the crowd. Nor would a setup be impossible this day, by any means, particularly in a nation that had earned a global reputation as a safe haven for felons on the run.

He counted seven people waiting for his fellow passengers, noting that none of them spared him more than a passing glance. His contact, according to Brognola, was supposed to meet him at the airport, but if something had gone wrong already, this soon in the game…

Bolan was a hundred feet from his arrival gate, eyeballing a sign that directed him to rental-car agencies and guessing that all would be closed, when a soft voice at his elbow said, "Matt Cooper?"

Bolan turned and blinked once at the lady, scanning her from head to toe in nothing flat before he said, "You have me at a disadvantage, Ms.…?"

"Blanca Herrera. And I doubt that very much."

Her grip was firm and strong as they shook hands. "You're late," she said. "No trouble on the flight, I hope?"

"Some kind of warning light came on, approaching Mexico City," Bolan replied. "They don't exactly set a land-speed record in the maintenance department."

"It was probably *siesta,* Señor Cooper. You're no longer in *El Norte.*"

"So I noticed."

"You have luggage?" she inquired.

"Just this," he said, hoisting his carry-on.

"A man who travels light. That's good."

"I still need wheels," he said.

"I know a good rental agency. An independent. We can use my car until morning and rent one then."

Bolan nodded. "And there's a man I need to see about some gear." A glance at his watch produced a frown. "He won't be open for a while yet."

"Have you slept?"

He nodded. "There was nothing else to do."

"Then breakfast," she said cheerily, "if that's agreeable."

"If you can find a place that's serving, I'm with you."

They cleared the terminal and Herrera led him underneath the floodlights to a parking lot. She handed him the keys. "If you wish to learn the city, it is best for you to drive."

"Sounds fair."

She took the shotgun seat and guided Bolan from the parking lot into sparse traffic. He followed her directions toward an all-night restaurant.

En route, she asked him, "May I know the nature of this gear that you require?"

"Hardware," he said, "in case I get into a tight place unexpectedly."

"And these would be illegal tools?"

"I haven't brushed up on the local statute books," he said, "but probably."

"I think I know the man you seek." She spoke a name and cocked one stylish eyebrow.

Bolan nodded. "That's the guy."

"You're right about his hours," Herrera said. "He operates a pawnshop as his—how you say it?—front."

"That's how we say it."

"Very good. Unfortunately, he does not open for business until nine o'clock in the morning. Can you do your other business then, as well?"

Bolan considered it. "It would be better after nightfall," he replied.

"Then you are graced with a free day in San José," she told him, putting on a smile that seemed a trifle forced. "If you allow me, and you have the energy after your flight, I'll be your tour guide."

"Sounds good," Bolan said, keeping both eyes on the road. "We'll start with target zones and access routes, then hit the culture afterward, if we have time."

3

San José
Wednesday, June 20

A bullet struck the rear of Bolan's rented vehicle and spent its force somewhere inside the trunk. Bolan stood on the accelerator, racing down the narrow alley, scattering trash cans in his wake.

The chase car's driver didn't seem to mind. He kept a lock on Bolan with his high beams, plowing through the refuse heaped across his path and battering aside the upended cans.

There were at least two shooters in the chase car, one in the front shotgun seat, another in the backseat, on the driver's side. Bolan knew that much only from their muzzle-flashes, since the high beams in his rearview mirror ruled out any head count.

Two guns minimum, and Bolan knew the driver would be armed, as well. The odds weren't bad, compared to some he'd faced.

Suddenly, a second pair of headlights joined the chase, behind the first pursuit car, gaining rapidly along the alley's dark and narrow track. Bolan ruled out police, because the second vehicle displayed no flashing lights, sounded no siren.

Beside him, Blanca Herrera swiveled in her seat, her face blanched by headlight beams. She watched the chase cars, while Gil Favor huddled in the backseat, offering the smallest target possible under the circumstances.

"Here they come!" Herrera advised him, as if she thought Bolan might be unaware of the pursuit.

"I see them," he replied. "Hang on."

Almost before she could react to that warning, they cleared the alley and he cranked the Ford into the sharpest left-hand turn he could manage, startling a pair of jaywalkers who squealed and ran for safety on the sidewalk. Gunfire echoed from the alley at his back, even before the first chase car emerged. The pedestrians went prone.

Bolan was making all the haste he dared on residential streets, watching the sidelines where his own headlights and those closing behind him cast distorted, moving shadows. Any one of them might mask a another late-night rambler, possibly a child, and Bolan had to balance that thought with the threat of death that rode his bumper. At the same time, if he drove *too* fast and lost control, smashed up the Ford, he and his passengers were facing sudden death, the failure of his mission.

Triumph for Antonio Romano.

"I need someplace where I can deal with this," he told Herrera. "Ideas?"

She blinked at him, eyes bright with fear, then said, "Maybe the riverfront? They have warehouses, docks. Few people at this hour. Also waste ground."

"Good."

Bolan was already speeding northward, in the general direction of the Rio Torres. All he had to do was stay the course and hope the gunners trailing him didn't get lucky with a bullet to his gas tank or a tire.

"Could you distract them for me?" he asked Herrera.

"What?"

"Shoot back."

His words seemed to confuse her for a moment, then she powered down her window, leaned into the wind-rush gale and fired a pistol shot at the nearer chase car. Bolan saw it swerve, the driver taken by surprise, losing acceleration just as Herrera fired again.

"Try for the radiator," Bolan called out to her.

"What?"

"Between the headlights!"

"Sí!"

She triggered two more shots, and while the chase car lost a bit more ground, Bolan had no idea if any of the bullets found their mark. Regardless, he took full advantage of the other driver's lapse and put more road between them, speeding through dark intersections with a silent prayer that there would be no damned fool driving with his lights off, no foot traffic crossing just as Bolan barreled past.

Gil Favor's neighborhood boasted some of the smallest street signs known to man, perhaps another mark of high-priced exclusivity. It was impossible to read the signs in the glare of his headlights, racing through the streets at speeds he normally reserved for freeway driving, while two carloads of assassins tried to run him down.

Instead, Bolan reviewed the street map he had memorized that afternoon, while they were killing time. He knew that he must be a good half mile below the riverfront, at least, but he was heading in the right direction, making decent time. If he could just—

The Ford's rear window suddenly imploded from a bullet's impact. Herrera bit off the greater part of an instinctive scream, while Bolan ducked and heard—or *felt*—the slug zip past his face. It struck his rearview mirror, sent it spinning to the floor somewhere, and drilled a neat hole through the windshield as it exited.

Now he was blind in back, except for side mirrors that shrank the chase cars down to toy size. He didn't need the printed warning that reflected objects May Be Closer Than They Seem.

"Give them a few more rounds," he ordered Herrera, guessing that she'd fired off roughly half her pistol's magazine already.

"Right!"

She scrambled to obey, as Bolan held the pedal down and waited for his first glimpse of the waterfront.

BLANCA HERRERA GRIMACED, mouthing silent curses as the wind from behind her whipped long hair around her face, stinging her eyes. It was already bad enough, men she had never met trying to murder her, without betrayal from her own hair in the bargain.

She had practiced often enough with her HK4 pistol to feel confident with stationary, inanimate targets, but this running battle through the streets of San José was something else entirely. In her wildest fantasies, Herrera had thought that if she ever tried to shoot another human being it would be in some classic *film noir* setting, possibly a city park at midnight or the murky hallway of a derelict motel.

The last thing she'd imagined, when she set out with Matt Cooper to retrieve his witness from a mansion in the heart of San José, had been a bullet-riddled car chase leading to *the riverfront*.

If they survived that long.

She saw more muzzle-flashes from the nearer chase car and replied with two rounds from her own weapon. The sharp reports, though swiftly blown away, still stung her ears. The target vehicle swerved jerkily, but once again she couldn't tell if either of her bullets had made contact.

In the excitement, Herrera had forgotten that she was supposed to count her shots. Had she fired six or seven? Since the pistol's slide was closed, she had at least one cartridge left before she had to fumble for the spare clip in her handbag.

Now the second car was gaining ground, trying to pass the first or pull abreast so that gunmen in both chase cars could fire at her and Cooper. Angry at the presumption of her enemies, Herrera triggered her first shot at the second car—and saw her pistol's slide lock open on an empty chamber.

"Damn it!"

She ducked back inside the Ford's window, wind-tangled hair obscuring her vision as she reached down for her purse. She'd dropped it on the floor between her feet, after they shoved Favor into the car, before their enemies had shown up and begun the chase.

She snatched the bag and opened it, rooting past wallet, lipstick, compact, facial tissues, hairbrush, searching for the one thing that might save her life. Of course the pistol's extra magazine had slithered to the very bottom of her bag, beside a jingling key ring.

She dumped the purse into her lap, snatched up the slim black magazine and let the other items spill between her legs, onto the floorboard. One touch of a button dropped the empty magazine out of her pistol's grip, and she replaced it, thumbed the catch to close its slide and put a live round in the chamber.

Ready.

I'll count this time, she thought, *and know when I run out of bullets.* When she was unarmed, helpless against her enemies.

"We're getting there," Cooper said from the driver's seat.

She knew he meant the riverfront, but couldn't say how far they'd traveled while she was exchanging gunshots with the enemy.

"I'll try again," she said, kicking the contents of her purse aside and turning toward her open window.

"Wait. How many rounds do you have left?" he asked her.

"Eight."

"What caliber?"

Another bullet struck the Ford, making her wince as she replied, "Three-eighty."

"Better save them for the main event," he said. "I can't replace them."

Main event, she thought. Kill or be killed.

"But if they overtake us—"

"Two blocks, tops," he promised her. "We ought to have some stretch then. See what happens."

As if answering his comment, two more bullets whispered through the broad rear window's vacant frame and punched holes through the windshield. Herrera was surprised that it did not collapse entirely.

With windows blown away or open, Herrera smelled the Rio Torres well before she saw it, with the docks along its southern bank. Another moment, and she saw warehouses where the merchant ships unloaded cargo seven days a week. Some also docked at night, she reasoned, but she saw no crews at work in the immediate vicinity.

What now? she wondered, startled when Matt Cooper answered her. She wasn't aware that she had spoken.

"Now we improvise," he said. "No rules. We need an edge of some kind, but I haven't found it yet."

Cooper had turned onto the waterfront. Behind them, Herrera saw the chase cars following.

Squeezing the pistol in her fist until her knuckles ached, she watched their enemies and told him, "I think we have run out of time."

"WE HAVE THEM NOW," Armand Casale said. The anger that had burned inside his gut during the chase was fading now, relaxing into satisfaction.

Killing was the best part, always.

"After them," Casale ordered, settling back into his seat as his driver stepped on the gas. Off to their left, the other chase car kept pace, both engines growling in the night.

Casale didn't know these people who had snatched his target out from underneath his very nose, killing a number of his people in the process. Given half a chance, he would've liked to question them at length, but something told him that they were not likely to surrender.

Fine.

Eliminating them would be the next-best thing—more satisfactory for him, in fact, than keeping them alive. Above all else, he had to carry out his main assignment and make sure Gil Favor's mouth was shut for good.

Casale carried a submachine gun manufactured from a Ruger Mini-14 automatic rifle, designated the AC-556F. It had a folding stock, unlike the parent weapon, and could fire full-auto or in 3-round-burst mode, using a custom brake to keep the muzzle from climbing. If he needed backup with a little extra kick, the stainless-steel Colt Anaconda in a shoulder rig below Casale's left arm ought to fit the bill.

Casale didn't care about the men he'd lost so far that evening. They were expendable, no friends of his, and could be easily replaced. Only his duty to Antonio Romano mattered at the moment, and that duty was to guarantee that prosecutors in New York would have no traitors to support their case against the Don.

The Rio Torres waterfront appeared to be deserted at that hour, no one to disturb them or to summon the police. Casale clutched his weapon as they sped along behind the bullet-scarred sedan, wondering whether any of the shots they'd fired so far had wounded Favor.

Maybe he was dead or dying even now, huddled inside the vehicle.

Be sure. And kill the others, too.

No witnesses.

It was a rule that always served Armand Casale well.

So far, he hadn't fired his weapon during the pursuit, but that would change as soon as they were close enough for him to reasonably guarantee a hit. He had spare magazines, along with other tools and weapons, but Casale hated wasting ammunition—hated wasting *anything,* in fact, except the people he was paid to waste.

And this time he was being paid quite well.

The bullet-pocked Ford was doing sixty miles per hour, based on the speedometer on Casale's own dashboard. Granted, his vehicle was stolen, like the other chase car, but its gauges seemed to function properly.

At that speed, his intended prey would soon run out of waterfront.

As if on cue, the unknown driver whom they were pursuing hit his brakes, the taillights flaring, while he whipped the steering wheel hard to his left. Casale knew it was the left, because the Ford spun to *his* left, tires shrieking as the sedan made a quick one-eighty and rocked to a halt, maybe a hundred yards in front of him.

Now, what the hell…?

The old guys back in Jersey called that fancy driving a bootlegger's turn, something from their whiskey-running days, before Casale's parents had been born. The faceless driver had a certain style, but what he didn't have was any hope of getting off the riverfront alive.

"Slow down," Casale told his wheelman. "Let's see what he's got in mind."

The driver slowed but didn't stop. The other chase car took its cue from Casale's, keeping pace.

"He wants to go down fighting," Luca offered from the backseat.

The faceless driver who had let Gil Favor live on borrowed time was revving his engine now. Not going anywhere, just goosing it, the way street racers do at traffic lights sometimes.

Was it a challenge? Casale wondered. Did he want to play a game?

Let's play a round of chicken, Casale thought. And I guarantee you I won't flinch.

Of course, it didn't really matter what the nameless driver wanted. Once they closed the gap a little more, Casale meant to kill the stranger and his passengers. His firing would unleash the other members of his crew, and they would turn the Ford into a giant colander.

Only a few more yards...

When they were almost there, the bullet-punctured Ford leaped forward and charged directly toward the narrow space between Casale's stolen chase car and its mate.

"IS THIS THE MAIN EVENT?" Blanca Herrera asked.

"This is what we've got," Bolan replied. "Soon as we're close enough, unload with everything you have."

Eight rounds, he thought. Not much, but maybe she'd get lucky. Maybe.

"Now!"

He stamped on the accelerator and released the parking brake. Some kind of gasping, squeaking noise came from Gil Favor, lying on the rear floorboards, then Bolan lost it in the clamor of his engine and their guns.

He held the Uzi SMG left-handed, his arm fully extended out the driver's window. Herrera had removed the sound-suppressor, at his direction, moments earlier. For the maneuver Bolan had in mind, he wanted noise and muzzle-flare, nothing to mute the submachine gun's lethal voice or spoil his aim with deadweight on the business end.

He held the Ford steady, no swerving, with the river on his left and two cars coming at him, high beams glaring in his face. Instead of shooting out those lights, he aimed above them and beyond the hoods that covered snarling engines, angling for the prize inside the package.

At his side, Herrera was squeezing off her eight rounds like a pro, not hurrying, and if he'd glanced in that direction, Bolan knew that he would find her aiming, eyes clenched nearly shut against the wind rushing in her face.

They started with a hundred yards between them and the two chase cars. As soon as Bolan charged them, both sedans came on to meet him. They weren't precise in their coordination, but he'd rate it close enough, better than most. There was a single brain behind the trap, and it was racing toward him now in one of the chase cars, while shooters started blazing at him from their open windows.

Bolan wondered who would flinch. In chicken, someone nearly always did—and if they didn't, someone nearly always died.

Bolan didn't intend to die this night, but he was at a disadvantage, playing off against two adversaries. If he folded, veered away at the last second, there was no way he could swerve around both chase cars and continue in the direction he was going now.

His choices, if they called his bluff, were right or left. Right led him to a warehouse loading dock, essentially a solid wall of concrete. Left would take him to the river and a deep, dark swim.

Don't flinch, he thought as wild rounds started clanging off and through the rented Ford sedan. Bolan milked short bursts from his Uzi, tried to make them count, vaguely aware of shiny brass spewing from the ejector port, bouncing across the Ford's sloped hood, some of the casings blowing back into the car through gaping holes in the windshield.

Herrera ran out of ammunition, cursing fluently in Spanish. Nothing more for her to do beyond that point, except to huddle underneath the dashboard, trying not to die.

Bolan heard more rounds strike the Ford, narrowed his eyes against a hail of pebbled safety glass as a bullet finally took out the spiderwebbed remainder of the windshield. Now the rush of wind in Bolan's face redoubled, and the sounds of gunfire from the two onrushing chase cars sounded twice as loud.

How long before *his* magazine ran dry?

Not long, though trying to count shots with automatic weapons was a waste of energy and precious, fleeting time.

He caught a break with one of his last six or seven rounds. The bullets found something beneath the sleek hood of the chase car on his left and struck a spark. It blew, a gust of smoke and fire that flung the hood backward, covering the chase car's windshield, rendering its driver blind.

His adversary had a choice: roll on and risk collision with a speeding car that might not swerve, or swing away from the vehicle on his left, off toward the water. When it swung away, trailing a plume of fire in its mad dash to find the water, Bolan steered his own ride through the sudden gap and let the other chase car pass him by at speed.

But that wasn't the end of it. It couldn't be.

Bolan hit the brakes again, got out and retrieved his larger duffel. He unzipped the bag, found the Steyor AUG assault rifle already loaded, and was waiting when the sole remaining chase car turned, preparing for a second pass.

He started firing when the other car was sixty yards away, its bodywork no match for 5.56 mm full-metal-jacketed rounds. Bolan took out the driver first, then killed his shotgun rider as the car began to lose momentum, drifting off course.

A shooter leaped out of the backseat with the car still moving, fired a wild pistol shot at Bolan and began to run for cover that he hadn't scouted yet.

He didn't make it.

Blanca Herrera had a dazed look on her face as Bolan slid into the driver's seat once more. Lips worked as she began to speak, but Bolan beat her to it.

"Hold that thought," he said. "We'll talk about it when we've found another car."

ARMAND CASALE NEVER wore a seat belt for precisely this reason. He'd rather pay a fine, if stopped by a policeman who was not on Don Romano's pad, than find himself trapped in a burning car.

Make that a *former* burning car, now sinking in a filthy river, pitch-black water pouring in around him through the open windows.

In the driver's seat, immediately to Casale's left, he had a brief glimpse of the wheelman just before they lost the light. The driver slumped against his shoulder harness, moving like a gruesome bobble-head as water swirled around him. Whether he was dead or just unconscious from the crash, Casale couldn't say.

Nor did he care.

The car was filling up, and it was each man for himself. Casale never gave a thought to grappling with the driver's belt, much less to dragging Luca from the backseat as the vehicle sank ever deeper, leaving air and any hope of life behind.

He left the submachine gun and his other gear inside the stolen car. Screw it. If there was trouble waiting at the surface, he still had the Anaconda in its shoulder harness and the WASP knife on his belt.

As always, he was dressed to kill.

Casale felt a flare of unfamiliar panic when he couldn't get his door open. The water pressure held it fast, defeating his best efforts, wasting vital seconds while his lungs began to ache for oxygen. He'd heard about that somewhere, definitely, but it had to have slipped his mind.

Cursing behind clenched teeth and lips, Casale wormed his way out through the open passenger's window, fighting the river's current and the drag of the sinking car. At first, Casale thought his shoulders were too broad to fit through the window. Then he led with his right hand while he pressed his chin down tight against his chest and nearly put his left ear on his shoulder.

That was better, but his belt snagged next on something that he couldn't see. Real panic clutched Casale's heart then, as he saw himself sucked down to icy death, trapped with his body half outside the vehicle, feeding the fish until only his bones remained.

He fumbled at his belt with one hand, then put both to work on it. Casale's lungs and throat were burning now, pinwheels of light cavorting on the insides of his eyelids. He was sinking, and increasing pressure threatened to expel whatever air remained inside his tortured lungs.

Then, suddenly, the vehicle released him, spit him out. Kicking frantically, Casale strained for the surface, nearly certain for a moment that his lungs would burst before he got there and his corpse would sink once more, trailing the car to find its resting place in silt and mud.

After the river's depths, the sudden flare of floodlights on the waterfront, some thirty yards away, drove needles deep into Casale's eyes. He gasped for air, thrashed toward the dock, swimming without a hint of style or grace. His stroke was functional, and that was all that mattered.

He reached the dock, clung to the pilings, scanned with bleary, burning eyes until he found a ladder at the water's edge. Casale dog-paddled to reach it, grasped the lower rung, then climbed with almost superhuman effort to dry land.

Sirens.

He couldn't tell how far away they were, or even if they were approaching, but they always meant bad news. Casale struggled to his feet, and at the same time saw the second carload of his soldiers waiting for him, less than forty feet away from where he stood.

Someone had shot the car to hell, along with everyone inside it. There was no point leaning in, leaving his fingerprints to check for pulses, when his men were obviously dead. The car still idled, burning gas but going nowhere with a corpse behind the wheel and two more on the side for company.

"Okay," Casale told the dead men. "Everybody out."

He took the driver first, unhooked his safety belt and dragged his corpse from the vehicle. It sounded like a sack of dirty laundry when it hit the pavement. Next, the backseat gunner, since Casale didn't have to walk around the car to reach him.

When he had two bodies on the deck, Casale climbed into the driver's seat and reached across the front-seat passenger, opening his door from the inside. A shove and kick unloaded him, leaving Casale in the car alone.

It was a bitch, sitting in blood and brains, but with his suit already trashed, what difference did it make? Escape was his priority, and in another moment he was on his way.

Next, ditch the wheels. Find more at any cost, then start the round of phone calls that, with any luck, could salvage something from disaster.

Now, before it was too late.

4

After the past two hours, Herrera's safehouse didn't feel so safe. It was an old two-bedroom place on Calle Ocho—Eighth Street—two long blocks from San José's main bus depot. The neighborhood was middle class by Costa Rican standards, meaning run-down homes on tiny lots, still light-years distant from the standard Latin American slum.

Before returning to the safehouse, they had gone in search of wheels. Bolan had picked a conservative sedan from the Hotel Corobici's self-serve parking lot, switched plates and hot-wired it, then let Herrera trail him while he dropped the Ford in the red-light district, key in the ignition.

It was a toss-up whether cops or thieves would find it first, a matter of complete indifference to Bolan as he thought about his trip back to the States.

A thought that didn't seem to please their guest.

"You can't do this," Favor insisted, seemingly undaunted by the fact that he was handcuffed to a chair. "You can't just kidnap someone from a foreign country, take him back to the United States and make believe that everything's in order."

"Really," Bolan said.

"Yes, *really,*" Favor snapped at him. "I know the mood in Washington, okay? The mighty U.S.A. gets anything it wants, and never mind the rules, but there are legal consequences. First, you have to get me out of Costa Rica, where I have more friends than you imagine."

"We met some of them tonight, I think," Bolan replied.

The captive shook his head. "I don't know who those bastards were, but if you killed them, then you spared them all some pain. The friends I mean are men who run this country. Get it? Judges.

Legislators. The commander of the national police. Some even higher on the food chain. Are you reading me?"

"I hear you," Bolan said. "You steal, then spread the loot around."

"It's called protection," Favor said.

"It didn't help you much tonight."

"Shit happens. You were helpful. I acknowledge that, and we can definitely make a deal. But this—" he paused and shook his handcuffs, rattling them "—won't get you anywhere."

"I guess we'll see."

"So, what's your plan, you and the pretty lady?" Favor asked. "Flying? My friends will have the airport covered. Ditto on the highways, if you're thinking you can drive me back through all those border checkpoints. Maybe we'll be sailing? Better keep an eye out for the coast guard."

"All those people mobilized for little you?" Bolan asked, goading him. He struck a nerve and saw the angry color rise in Favor's cheeks.

"I may seem little to you now, old son," the swindler growled, "but when you've had a few nights in a dungeon, under round-the-clock interrogation, maybe I'll stop by and see how big you feel. If you're alive."

"That's scary," Bolan said.

"Okay. I tried to help you," Favor said. "Go on and bluff it out. There's nothing I can do for you."

"So, how about helping yourself?"

The fugitive examined Bolan as if he were some peculiar specimen unknown to modern science, then said, "I don't get you."

Bolan shrugged. "You're so concerned about my welfare, but it hasn't been two hours since a hit team tried to take you out. Maybe that slipped your mind in the debate about your civil rights."

Another shrug from Favor, unconvincing. "I leave all that to my friends. They handle any problems that arise."

"I didn't see them anywhere around your place tonight," Bolan reminded him. "Some kind of holiday?"

"They're only human."

"So are you," Bolan said. "You may have a couple billion dollars up your sleeve, but you still bleed and die like anybody else."

"Who doesn't? Look, for all I know, you staged that row tonight with actors firing blanks. Last time around, the IRS auditioned hookers, hoping one of them would drug me. Then a *rescue* team would come along and whisk me off to safety at the U.S. Embassy. Of course, the smart whores came to me and got a double payday."

"What about the others?" Bolan asked him.

"There was only one who took the bait. She had some legal problems, I believe. Something about narcotics and sedition." Favor turned his gaze on Herrera. "You can't imagine what goes on in women's prisons hereabouts—or can you?"

Her face remained deadpan.

"And you risk all of that," Favor said, "just to take me back for trial on what, a few counts of embezzlement? Give me a break. Assuming that the charges aren't dismissed because of your illegal actions—which they *will* be—what's the worst that I could get? Five years? With good behavior, I'll be out in eighteen months. Ready to fly back here, or somewhere else, and settle in the lap of luxury."

"Sorry, you lost me there," Bolan replied. "Who said we're holding you for trial?"

GIL FAVOR FELT a little chill snake down his spine. Although he knew it was impossible, the handcuffs seemed to tighten just a little on his wrists.

"Excuse me?"

The tall stranger, who had yet to introduce himself, regarded Favor as if he were so much baggage, packed and ready for the moving van.

"We're not concerned about your sticky fingers," he replied. "That's someone else's job."

Confused, Favor demanded, "So, who are you, then?"

"Your new best friends."

"I hardly think so."

"Then ask yourself who wants you dead," the tall man said. "And if that list's too long to wrap your mind around, consider who might want you dead right now."

Favor considered it and came up blank. He kept his mouth shut, reckoning that silence was his safest bet.

The tall man frowned. "I don't suppose Antonio Romano rings a bell?"

"Romano?" Favor caught himself, regained his self-control in time to save it. Shifting on the chair that held him prisoner, he tried to strike a careless pose. "Sorry," he said. "It doesn't ring a bell."

"That's odd," his captor said. "Romano's shooters almost rang your bell tonight. But you have no idea why they'd be gunning for you?"

"Since I've never heard of this Romano person, no, I can't imagine. On the other hand, you may be picking names out of thin air, to wind me up."

"What good would that do anybody?" the stranger asked. "If you never met Romano, there's no reason he should try to silence you before his trial. Must be some mistake. Unfortunate for you, though."

Favor blinked twice, then restrained himself before it turned into a nervous tic. "You're saying this Romano person is on trial?" he asked.

"Will be," the tall man answered. "The proceedings were delayed. Seems like the witnesses keep dying."

"Just to satisfy my idle curiosity," Favor said, "what's the charge against him?"

"Charges, plural. I don't have the list in front of me, but I remember racketeering, murder, arson and some kind of a conspiracy involving foreign terrorists."

Favor could feel the blood leaving his face. For just a moment he was dizzy, then he managed to regain a bit of his composure. "Foreign terrorists? Now I'm convinced you've lost your mind. Can we speak frankly here?"

"I'd call it a refreshing change," his captor said.

"All right, then. I'm a thief, okay? I've always been a thief. I like money and all the things that I can buy with it. I'm greedy, but I'm not political. I *buy* airplanes and yachts—I don't hijack them. You are barking up the wrong tree, friend."

"Romano doesn't seem to think so."

"Screw Romano! What is it you think I've done?"

The tall man shrugged. "I wasn't briefed on details. Something worth a dirt nap, from Romano's point of view. He obviously wants to shut you up for good, before you get to court and rain on his parade."

"Two problems there," Favor replied. "First, I won't *be* in court. And second, even if I was, I wouldn't testify."

"I'm only handling the delivery," his captor said. "As far as any testimony goes, I have a feeling that Romano would prefer to guarantee your silence the old-fashioned way."

"This is ridiculous," Favor said. "I can promise you you'll never get me out of Costa Rica. Let me go right now—I'll make it worth your while. What do you say? A million each, in cash?"

His jailers glanced at each other, then their eyes came back to Favor. "Thanks, but no thanks," said the man.

"All right, I tried," Favor said. "It's your funeral."

"We might surprise you."

"No," Favor replied. "Surprising me would mean you did the smart thing. Take the money, let me go and live a little. But you're cops. And cops aren't very smart, in my experience."

"Does that include the ones you bought down here?"

"Don't get me wrong, friend," Favor said. "They recognize their own best interest, and I've paid them well. That's why they won't let you go back to Washington or wherever the hell you plan on going with the golden goose."

"You got that wrong," the tall man said.

"Excuse me?"

"You said 'the golden goose.' That's wrong. It was the goose that laid the golden eggs. When it runs out of gold, it's just another goose. Another Sunday dinner."

"I've got golden eggs enough to last a hundred lifetimes," Favor said. "Don't worry about that."

"But when Romano's people take you out, who's going to deliver? Think about it. Chances are, Romano has already cut a deal with your amigos here in San José. You know as well as anybody that the highest bidder claims their loyalty."

Favor shook his head. "I don't believe it."

"Either way," the tall man said, "we'll find out soon enough."

Washington, D.C.
2:45 a.m.

"I HOPE THIS IS important," Hal Brognola said.

The bedside telephone had jarred him from a deep sleep.

"I'd say it is," Mack Bolan's voice replied.

"How's it going?" Brognola inquired, immediately wide-awake.

"We have the package," Bolan said, "but we encountered some resistance at the pickup site."

"I see."

He didn't, really, but no great imagination was required to picture the resistance Bolan had in mind, and they could not discuss the details on an open line.

"Is everyone okay?" Brognola asked. "Yourself and your assistant? What about the package?"

"All intact," Bolan assured him. "After the initial problem, some negotiation was required, but I'm on top of it and looking forward to delivery on schedule, one way or another."

So, Gil Favor either had resisted or was still resisting transport to the States. They'd all anticipated that. If necessary, Bolan had a sedative on hand in quantities sufficient to keep Favor dreaming all the way from San José to the U.S.

"Ready for pickup, then?" the big Fed asked.

"Considering the weather," Bolan answered, "we've decided that it's best to go commercial. All that bad publicity about the private jets and fuel efficiency, the global-warming thing. You know the drill."

Brognola read between the lines of Bolan's seemingly innocuous remarks. For "global warming," he read *heat,* the kind that made it risky even for a charter flight or U.S. military jet to whisk Favor out of Costa Rica. All the cops and politicians, customs agents, soldiers whom Favor had been paying off for years on end to keep him safe were now on full alert, prepared to earn their money.

"Well, if you think that commercial is the way to go," Brognola said, "I trust your judgment."

Not that he had any choice. Bolan would know the risks of ferrying his hostage to the States on a civilian aircraft. Stripped of any weapons and surrounded by potential enemies, including members of the flight crew. During any stops, if they deplaned, each crowded airport terminal would present dozens of possible death traps.

"Okay, then," Bolan said. "I haven't booked a flight yet, but I'll call and leave a message from the airport when it's all arranged. Maybe someone can meet me at the other end?"

"Count on it," Brognola replied.

He'd have the whole damned FBI field office on hand to welcome Bolan and Favor, every G-man and -woman armed to the teeth, if that was what it took to keep the witness breathing and deliver him on schedule to the witness stand.

Brognola didn't even want to think about Romano skating on the present list of charges, when the Justice team had worked so hard to link his family to global terrorists. The effort had consumed thousands of person-hours, spread over eighteen months, and it had cost the life of one young agent who got too close to the fire.

Of course, there was another way to handle it, if charges were dismissed or if misguided jurors voted to acquit. Brognola could've gone that route in the beginning, put a word in Bolan's ear and watched the act unfold, but he still cherished faith in the America of grade-school civics lessons, where the courts dispensed justice without regard for wealth, influence or the rest of it.

"I'll be in touch, then," Bolan said. "And see you at the other end."

Brognola answered, "Right. If I hear anything you need to know, I'll reach out to your sat phone."

"Roger that," Bolan said, and the line went dead.

Brognola rose and stretched. Someone was always wide-awake and working at the Farm. He needed to alert them, set a watch on flights departing Costa Rica for the States and have the crucial welcome mat in place when Bolan landed with the witness.

Doing everything that he could do to make it safe and simple, even though the Justice man's gut told him it likely wouldn't help.

San José

"WILL HE GO THROUGH with it?" Blanca Herrera asked.

They'd left Gil Favor handcuffed to his chair and settled in another room to talk, where they wouldn't be overheard.

Matt Cooper shrugged. "He's getting on the plane, no matter what. I can sedate him if I have to, all the way. He has no choice."

"And when he gets there?" she persisted.

"As I told him, my part's the delivery. I naturally hope he'll do his civic duty on the witness stand. But do I trust him? Not as far as I can throw this house."

His answer confirmed Herrera's personal fears. "You expect trouble then, at the airport?"

"Anything's possible," Cooper replied. "Favor could make a scene. More shooters could be waiting for us. We could even hit a snag with your people."

"*My* people?" Herrera challenged him.

Cooper seemed not to notice her reaction. "Customs agents, the police," he said. "Whoever's taking money from our boy in there to cover him."

Herrera was painfully familiar with her homeland's reputation when it came to harboring the scum of Europe and America. Before she went into police work, she'd considered leaving altogether, but her roots were deep in Costa Rican soil, and she still hoped that young idealists like herself could someday change the system, purge it of corruption and restore the country's reputation.

Someday.

In the meantime, it still rankled when professionals like Cooper viewed her fellow officers with a suspicion verging on contempt. And it pained Herrera all the more to know that their distrust was frequently well-founded.

Haltingly, she said, "I hope you don't think I...I mean to say..."

"Don't sweat it," Cooper said. "If you were dirty, you'd have made your move by now."

"Is that a vote of confidence?" she asked.

"Could be."

"At least you don't waste time on flattery."

He smiled at that, for nearly two full seconds. "Like you just said, it's a waste of time. I count on a professional to do her job without warm fuzzies every time she doesn't drop the ball."

"What are these 'warm fuzzies'?" Herrera inquired.

"It's slang for compliments," Cooper responded. "Pros perform on demand, every time. They don't need someone patting their backs when they do a job right. It's expected."

"So praise is superfluous, then?"

"Oh, it's great, in exceptional cases," Cooper said. "Service above and beyond the call, and all that. It's why armies give medals for valor. The good-conduct pins aren't worth much."

"And if you manage to deliver this one—" she nodded toward the adjacent room "—will you get warm fuzzies then?"

"I wouldn't count on it. It's what I was assigned to do."

"Then you move on to something else?"

"That's right," he said. "Like you."

"My work is always here, in San José."

"Same thing," Cooper said. "You move on from one case to another, right? You don't expect the brass to throw a party every time you carry out a simple order."

"No. But this one, I believe, is not so simple."

Cooper shrugged again. "So far, it's been more or less what I expected."

"And the killing? Was this also what you thought would happen? Is it how you live?"

"It's how I stay alive sometimes," he said. "Dealing with terrorists and with the Mafia, it's SOP."

"Again, the slang," she chided him.

"Standard operating procedure," Cooper translated.

"I see." Herrera considered reaching out to him, but then thought better of it. "And I am sorry."

"For what?"

"That you lead such a life."

"Could be worse," Cooper said. "Like not living."

"Tonight, when we—"

"Let's talk about the airport," Cooper said, cutting her off. "If Favor plays along, we'll walk him in. If not, we'll need to make special arrangements for an invalid who's basically unconscious. I'll play doctor if we have to go that route."

"And I will be your nurse," she said.

"You only work in San José, remember?" Cooper asked.

"Professionals do as they're told, you said," she countered. "I was ordered to assist you in completion of your work. There was no mention of abandoning you at the airport."

"You should look into that," he said, "before you take a leap of faith and wind up jumping out of your career. My people won't assume responsibility for any rash decisions."

"They are *my* decisions," she replied. "*I* will assume responsibility. Now, shall we go and find out if we have a traveling companion or a patient, Dr. Cooper?"

FAVOR SURPRISED BOLAN by falling into line with the suggested plan, minus the tranquilizers and restraints. Bolan made no attempt to keep the skepticism off his face.

"Hey, don't look so surprised," the swindler said. "I had some time to think while you were chatting in the other room. I hate to say it, but you may be right. Romano can outspend me in the short-term, and it's only logical the natives would jump ship if they believe I'm going down." He flashed a microsecond smile at Herrera then, and added, "No offense."

"None taken," she responded icily.

"Well, damn it. Now I've hurt your feelings," Favor said.

"That is of no concern to you."

"It is, as long as you're half of the team that's keeping me alive," he said. "How can I make it up to you?"

"You can desist from further insults," she replied. "That would include the bribe you are about to offer."

"Now *I'm* hurt."

Bolan cut through the small talk. "Listen up," he said. "I need to book our reservations. Then, depending on our flight time, we can judge how long it takes to pack and go."

"I hate to state the obvious," Favor said, "but I have nothing to pack and no passport. It's all at home, presumably now occupied by the police."

"I have your new passport," Bolan replied. "Your name is Edward Janeway, and you live in New York City. You've been traveling in Costa Rica for the past two weeks, with all the necessary stamps to prove it."

"So, you've thought of everything—including luggage, I presume?"

"We have an extra bag of clothes," Bolan said.

"Please, no tweed or polyester!"

"Size and style don't matter, since you won't be wearing any of it. Something for security to check, so we don't cause suspicion."

"Which must mean I won't be wearing these," Favor said as he gently set the handcuffs rattling.

"No," Bolan agreed. "If I believe restraints are necessary at the airport or aboard the flight, I'll dip into my doctor's bag."

"Licensed to practice, are we?" Favor asked.

"My paperwork's in order," Bolan said. "Just like your passport."

"Ah. But if you're shaky, even just a little, I might get an overdose."

"That's something else to think about before you break our deal," Bolan said.

Favor looked insulted. "I assure you, I am a man of my word."

"Uh-huh. I'll keep the needles handy, just in case."

"O, ye of little faith."

"Try no faith, and you've hit it on the head." He turned to Herrera. "Have you got him while I make the reservations?"

"Why don't I do that?" she asked. "It will be easier, in Spanish."

Bolan met her gaze, studied the lady for another moment and then made his own leap of faith. "Sounds all right," he replied. "Go ahead."

She offered him a quick smile, then went off to use the telephone.

"Oh, sure," Favor said from his chair. "You trust the woman."

"Why not?" Bolan replied. "She hasn't stolen anything that I'm aware of, and she's not a fugitive."

"Throw that up in my face, why don't you?"

"All you need to think about," Bolan said, "is our deal. I take for granted that you have a few tricks up your sleeve, but they won't help. Worst-case scenario, you get away from me and find Romano's shooters waiting for you. I can promise you, they won't negotiate."

"And if I go along…?"

"Play straight with me," Bolan continued, "and you travel upright, under your own power. At the first sign of disruption, you're sedated and you wake up in the States."

"What can I say? I've agreed already. Can we lose the cuffs?"

"Not yet. I'll ditch them at the airport. After that…"

"I know. The needle's waiting. Say no more—I get the point."

You will, Bolan thought, if you try to play me for a fool.

5

San José International Airport
June 20

The airport was crowded when Bolan and Herrera arrived with Gil
Favor, forty minutes prior to their departure time. They'd cut it close
on purpose, hoping thus to minimize exposure to police or any other
searchers in the terminal itself.

Bolan had left their stolen ride in long-term parking, with his
military hardware locked inside the trunk. It could be days or weeks
before someone discovered it, depending on the relative efficiency
of airport security forces. He kept the keys in his pocket, prepared
to ditch them on the plane before he disembarked.

Security inside the terminal was relatively lax, compared to what
Bolan had experienced when flying out of the U.S. They X-rayed
carry-ons, of course, and had the passengers troop through a metal
detector the size and shape of an old-fashioned phone booth, but
there was no removing shoes or jackets, no pat-downs unless the
shrill alarm on the detector singled someone out as suspect.

Bolan passed the check with flying colors, since the sedative syrettes
that he'd concealed upon his person were the latest in high-impact
plastic technology. A twist-off cap revealed a short but sturdy plastic
needle, and the knockout dose behind it was triggered on impact. One
dose would put a large man down for several hours. Two might keep
him down for good, depending on his age and general health.

Favor had promised not to make a scene, and he kept his word
from their presentation of passports at the ticket counter through the
final security checkpoint. Well-armed police were on patrol through-

out the terminal, and Favor could have brought them running with a wave or shout, but he stayed quiet all the way.

Bolan tried to imagine what was going on in Favor's mind. Had he accepted the reality that staying in Costa Rica meant Romano's men would kill him on their next attempt, or the one after that? Was he resigned to bargaining for favors, based upon the value of his testimony in New York? Or was he working some other angle that was still obscure?

In any case, Bolan knew better than to trust the man who'd made a megafortune lying to investors, friends and family, the government and everybody else who knew him. Bolan wouldn't have believed Gil Favor if the man had sworn an oath that he was lying.

After passing through security, they still had fifteen minutes left before their flight was due to board. Five minutes into that countdown, Favor began to fidget in his seat, making small sounds suggestive of distress.

At last he told them, "Sorry, people. I don't know if it's my nerves or what. I need to hit the men's room."

"Hold it," Bolan said, "until we're in the air."

"Easy for you to say," Favor replied, speaking through clenched teeth as he crossed his legs. "You're not the one about to blow."

"We don't have time."

"Come on. The restrooms are right over there." Favor pointed to a pair of doors marked with the universal male and female figures. Bolan estimated they were thirty feet away from where he sat.

"Too late," he said.

"Okay," Favor said. "You're the boss. But in case you're wrong you'll want to have a story ready for the flight attendants to explain the way I smell. You think they'll let me take a load on board?"

Damn it!

"All right," Bolan relented. "Come with me."

"A twosome? Listen, I can handle this myself. Been doing it for years, and—"

"It's a double team or nothing," Bolan answered. "Take it or leave it."

"I'll take it," Favor said, "before I explode."

Herrera remained behind to hold their seats and watch their carry-ons, while Bolan escorted Favor to the lavatory.

Passing from the concourse proper onto antiseptic-smelling tile, Bolan scanned the men's room for patrons and saw only two. An older, portly man was finishing his business at the urinal farthest from the entrance, while a pair of legs was visible beneath the half door of the bathroom's central stall.

Gil Favor made a beeline for the first stall, leaving one empty between himself and the silent meditator. The other man stepped up to wash his hands, and Bolan did likewise, a time killer that let him watch the toilet stalls reflected in a mirror set above the sinks.

Bolan was getting curious about the hombre in the other stall. Unlike Favor, he made no sounds and didn't seem to move at all. Was he asleep in there? Reading a book to pass the time before his flight in privacy? If he'd suffered a stroke or heart attack, Bolan assumed he would've tumbled off the throne, but—

Favor flushed his toilet, spent a moment straightening his clothes, then stepped out of the stall. "That's a load off my mind," he declared, "if you know what I mean."

Chuckling at his own wit, the fugitive washed his hands quickly and dried them with three paper towels before turning to Bolan.

"So, hey," he inquired, "are we ready to go?"

THE PLAN HAD COME to Favor as he sat on the commode. It might not work, but what else could he do? Returning to the States, much less New York, was tantamount to suicide. At least he had a chance in Costa Rica, and if all else failed he knew that he could run again, start over with his money somewhere else.

But first he needed to break free of his two escorts.

Favor saw the cops as he approached the threshold of the men's room. There were two of them in starched green uniforms, with submachine guns slung across their chests and belts heavy with other lethal-looking gear. One of them glanced at Favor, and he seized the golden opportunity.

Turning to face his escort, Favor shoved the larger man and

simultaneously raised his voice, shouting in Spanish, "That's disgusting! Keep away from me!"

His escort cursed, was reaching for an inside jacket pocket when he saw the officers approaching, hands on weapons. As the uniforms drew nearer, Favor moved to intercept them, telling them—again, in Spanish—that this total stranger had approached him in the men's room with a vile, infuriating proposition. If the lawmen doubted Favor's word, they'd find another witness in the lavatory.

One of them peeled off to check the men's room, while the other started asking Favor's captor questions in rapid-fire Spanish. A crowd of onlookers had gathered and was growing by the moment, pressing close to find out what was happening.

Favor knew that he had only a moment, maybe less, before the woman clicked to what was happening and tried to head him off. Never a fighter, Favor wasn't sure that he could overpower her, especially if she was trained in unarmed combat. Either way, however, grappling with her in the middle of the concourse, while police were standing by, would foil his getaway.

He stepped back from the cop and his unwelcome escort, elbowing his way between the rubberneckers. No one tried to stop him, since they wanted ringside seats, and anyone retreating from the center of the action gave them better access. Half a dozen backward steps, and then the crowd thinned out. Others were moving in to join the crush, and that was fine with Favor. They would screen him from the cop, not giving him a second glance.

Public indecency with only men involved could be a fairly serious offense in Costa Rica, where the church still kept its grip on public attitudes toward sex and immorality. It was a rude surprise for someone who had saved his life just hours earlier, but Favor wasn't one for sentiment.

Besides, the cop's whole case would fall apart the minute he glanced back and saw that his complaining witness had evaporated.

Favor wasn't going back to New York City, period. Case closed. He hadn't known why Tony Romano would want him dead until the big man mentioned terrorists, and then it all came crashing down on Favor with a vengeance. In that moment, he had known that there was nothing he could tell Romano that would get him off the hook.

Gil Favor was as good as dead, unless he found another hiding place. And New York wasn't it.

He cleared the last row of the growing crowd and started walking. Pent-up tension made him want to run, but that would be the giveaway, especially with two more officers approaching, just ahead of him. Favor looked past them, putting on the very face of innocence that he had used to lull investors, business partners, friends and friends of friends.

It almost never failed.

What now?

His situation was extreme, verging on desperate, but Favor still had hope. His first task was to put the damned airport behind him, find some temporary shelter and reach out to those who owed him service for the wealth that he had poured into their pockets.

Favor had the most important numbers memorized, as a survival reflex. After one or two calls, he would know which way the wind was blowing, whether he could trust his purchased friends or not. If they were edgy, tried to put him off, Favor would bide his time, retrieve his secret cache of spending money once his bank opened and he could tap his safe-deposit box.

From there, with cash in hand, he could go anywhere. Another country or another continent, it made no difference. He could access his bank accounts in San José from anywhere on Earth that had a telephone or Internet connection. Transfer of the money was as easy as a keystroke.

But he had to choose a hiding place, and choose it well.

Gil Favor knew that he was walking on a razor's edge, with sudden death on every side. And if he didn't get it right this time, there'd be no second chance.

BLANCA WAS THUMBING through a magazine when angry voices made her glance back toward the restrooms. Instantly, she felt a surge of panic as she saw the two policemen moving toward Gil Favor and

Matt Cooper. Favor was saying something that she couldn't quite make out.

Whatever accusation he had made, the officers appeared to take it seriously. One of them was asking Cooper questions now, the other moving briskly toward the men's room.

Why?

She rose, taking her magazine along with her, and drifted toward the scene of confrontation. Herrera kept it casual, no rushing, moving with the other airport travelers who might be running late for flights but who could not resist a bit of real-life controversy on the way.

As she approached, she caught a warning glance from Cooper, coupled with a subtle movement of his head from side to side. He didn't want her joining in the argument, whatever it might be. She turned, focused on Favor and observed him slipping backward through the press of onlookers.

Bastard.

She knew at once what he had done, some silly charge against Matt Cooper that would keep him busy with police while Favor slipped away and vanished. The swindler wouldn't give his real name, wouldn't mention kidnapping or murder, on the off chance that authorities had turned against him and might hand him over to his would-be killers.

Favor would hope she hadn't seen him yet, or that she'd stay with Cooper to try to sort out the problem as expeditiously as possible. Like every other man she'd known since childhood, he had under-estimated her.

She turned away from Cooper, guessing that the officers would let him go directly, when they found Favor was gone. That in itself would cast suspicion on his charges and preclude Cooper's arrest.

Herrera hurried around the crowd's expanding fringe, a counter-clockwise sweep that had her dodging bodies, giving some of them an elbow or a shoulder if they weren't quick enough to let her pass. Some muttered curses at her back, but she ignored them.

Where was Favor? She couldn't see him in the press of eager spectators. She knew he wasn't staying to discuss the matter with police. He didn't care if Cooper went to jail or not, as long as Favor had a chance to—

There?

She saw him moving at a brisk walk back in the direction they had come from upon entering the terminal. She thought about the stolen car and guns inside it, then remembered Cooper had the keys.

Favor would wish to leave the airport, get as far away from it as possible. For that he needed wheels, but he had empty pockets. They had seen to that, as a security precaution.

So he couldn't board a bus, but he could always hail a taxi, give the driver some address, then promise payment on arrival. Say his wallet was inside the house or someone else was there to pay the bill. It might result in trouble, but he'd take that chance. Better a scuffle on some street far distant from the airport than a confrontation in the airport concourse, with police on hand.

Herrera walked faster, lengthening her strides, though she was still afraid of running. It was better not to draw attention, more particularly since it seemed that Favor hadn't seen her yet. He had to think she was still with Cooper, maybe arguing with the police, and thereby giving him a chance to flee.

She had closed the gap between herself and Favor to some thirty yards when he glanced back and saw her, blinking rapidly in stark surprise. Herrera resisted the impulse to charge at him, swinging and kicking. It was best, she knew, if she could capture him without a scene that would attract more officers and onlookers.

Favor veered to his left, into a narrow corridor with signs mounted outside. The symbols on those signs promised more lavatories, public telephones, a water fountain.

Herrera reached the hallway just in time to see the men's-room door swing shut. She wondered if there was another exit from the room, or if her quarry hoped to wait her out, devise a better strategy while sitting on the toilet.

Without a vestige of embarrassment, Blanca Herrera shoved the swinging door and followed him inside.

THE COP WITH THE mustache and surly attitude began by challenging Bolan in rapid-fire Spanish. Clearly unimpressed with Bolan's answers in Spanish, the cop then shifted to awkward English after he'd wasted a full precious minute. It had been time enough for Favor to evaporate, while Bolan was reduced to beaming angry thoughts at Herrera, hoping that she'd notice and go after him.

The accusation, when it came, was more or less what Bolan had expected. "You try to touch this hombre in the *banyo* like he say, *señor?*"

Instead of arguing the point and reinforcing the cop's revulsion, Bolan looked around the ring of faces that encircled him and asked, "What hombre? Where'd he go?"

The cop swiveled his head and began to sputter curses in his native language. Just then, his companion came back from the men's room with another man whose shoes and trouser cuffs Bolan immediately recognized.

A round of heated questions left the fellow from the toilet stall shaking his head and pleading ignorance of any criminal offense. The officers released him, just as Bolan heard a disembodied female voice announce that first-class passengers were free to board his flight.

Damn it!

Both cops now turned their full attention back to Bolan, while he carefully concealed his fuming anger. The mustache said, "We want no funny business in the airport, understand? No funny business anywhere in San José."

"You need to find that other guy and make him stop accusing people."

"Oh, we find him," the mustache told Bolan as he turned away, scowling. "We find him pretty soon, you bet."

Unless I find him first, Bolan thought. Glancing at the row of seats where he'd left Herrera, Bolan found them filled with other bodies, other faces. He could only hope that she'd seen Favor slip away and had pursued him, maybe even overtaken him by now.

And then what?

Bolan struck off in the same direction Favor had been headed. Behind him, all around him, the seductive woman's voice announced the general boarding of his flight.

Favor could be anywhere by now, he realized. The airport wasn't huge by U.S. standards, but its teeming concourse offered countless places where a person could hide, plus many exits. If Herrera *hadn't* followed Favor, if she'd let him slip away somehow...

You can't blame her, whatever happens, Bolan told himself.

He had been suckered, pure and simple, and the fact that he was dealing with a proved scam master did nothing to relieve Bolan's embarrassment. Now, with his aircraft boarding, he was swiftly running out of time in which to rectify the situation.

If Bolan hadn't found his man within the next few minutes—his man and Herrera—then the plane would be departing with at least three empty seats.

Bolan scanned faces as he moved along the concourse, double-checking those that were averted suddenly. There were enough anglos scattered throughout the flowing crowd that Bolan reckoned he was bound to miss some.

And he only had to miss one for the plan to fail.

He saw Herrera in the same instant that the haunting, hellish voice broadcast their final boarding call. "All passengers should be aboard the aircraft at this time," the voice said.

Bolan moved forward on an interception course, hoping that Herrera could at least direct him to a new search quadrant. Then a family of nine or ten shifted enough to offer Bolan a glimpse of Favor, his right arm locked firmly in Herrera's left. The runner's face looked pale and sickly. Every shuffling step he took seemed painful.

"What happened to him?" Bolan asked.

"He tried to lose me in the lavatory," she replied. "Then, when I followed him, he tried to overpower me."

"I guess it didn't work."

"All men are fragile in the same vicinity," she told him, smiling. "What about our flight?"

"Too late," Bolan informed them both. "We missed it."

"YOU CAN'T BLAME ME for trying," Favor told the tall man as he huddled in his chair, a picture of misery.

"Oh, no? Just watch me."

"I've been punished by your dominatrix, anyway," the swindler whined. "There's nothing worse that you can do."

"Again, a challenge that you'd be wise not to make," his captor said.

The row of hard, uncomfortable seats they occupied faced a giant window and the runways out beyond it. Favor did what he could to ease the raw pain in his privates, where the woman's knee had solidly connected—twice.

"An ice pack would be much appreciated," Favor told them.

"Maybe later," said the grim man on his left.

"And maybe not," the woman on his right added.

"I don't see why we have to watch the bloody plane take off," Favor complained.

"We're killing time," Bolan replied. "We need another flight, new reservations with a special booking for a coma patient."

"Wait, now," Favor said, recoiling from the man, then stopping short when his female companion stuck a sharp elbow into his ribs. "That really isn't necessary."

"You were warned," Bolan reminded him. "You blew it."

"Try to look at it from *my* side," Favor said.

"Shut up and watch the plane you could've ridden like a man. The next one, you'll be traveling as checked luggage."

Favor sat and glowered at the runway. Their jet taxied onto the final stretch of tarmac, then started rolling forward, gaining speed with every yard it traveled. Near the runway's midpoint, Favor saw its nose lift, rising, and—

A blast of smoke and flame erupted just behind the starboard wing. Within a second, two at most, the fire ballooned, enveloping the rear half of the plane. Meanwhile, the forward section kept on rising, separated from the rest, like an artillery projectile.

It was airborne for another two or three seconds, before its climb became a backward somersault. When it came down, the forward section of the plane was upside down, its nose pointing back toward the fiery wreckage of its rear half. It came apart on impact, and was consumed by rolling, searing flames that devoured everything.

Favor felt vomit rising in his throat. He jackknifed forward, retching for the second time that morning. This time, it was unconnected to the throbbing ache between his legs. Sheer horror, and the knowledge that he'd nearly been among those flaming rag dolls on the tarmac, tied his stomach into knots and wrung it dry.

The spasm passed, and Favor felt hands lifting him on either side. His escorts hoisted him out of his seat and led him to a water fountain, where he stooped and rinsed the foul taste from his mouth. By slow degrees, as panic spread around them in the concourse, Favor found that he could stand up straighter, walk with less assistance from the bookends flanking him.

"Funny how things work out, eh?" he asked no one in particular. "If I'd been nice and docile, we'd be dead right now."

The tall man didn't seem to hear him. "I don't buy the coincidence," he told the woman.

"It's impossible," she said. "To have a bomb on board the aircraft, it would mean—"

"They're either psychic or they've got someone inside," Bolan replied. "Did you call anyone?"

The lady shook her head.

"Then it's on my end, damn it. I reported our itinerary."

"What do we do now?" she asked.

"Get out of here," Bolan said. "Take the car back. We can think about it on the road."

"I hate to be a naysayer," Favor said, "but is it possible, in light of what's just happened, that they may have someone covering the car?"

"It's possible," the Executioner admitted, "but it's still our best way out, unless you like the thought of walking all the way unarmed."

"We're driving now?" Favor asked. "All the way to Mexico?"

"We drive until we have a better plan," Bolan corrected him. "If you've got one ready, I'm happy to consider it."

"Unfortunately, no," Favor replied. "I'm tapped."

"The car it is, then," Bolan stated. "If you're up to it."

"Let's say I'm motivated," Favor answered. "Lead the way."

6

"Whose bright idea was it to bomb the plane?" Armand Casale asked. His tone implied that he already knew the question's answer.

Haroun al-Rachid's face was deadpan as he said, "I judged that it would be the most efficient method for achievement of our goal."

"You've seen the morning news?" Casale pressed. "About how well your plan worked out, I mean?"

The Saudi wore his usual arrogant expression, tempting Casale to slap him. "It all went according to schedule," he said. "The aircraft was destroyed on takeoff."

"And have you heard the body count, by any chance?"

The two men stood together in the study of a fair-size house Casale had rented on short notice by doubling the neighborhood's asking price. He liked the place, but hated sharing it with Arabs from the Sword of Allah. Still, when Don Romano ordered something to be done a certain way…

"At last report," al-Rachid answered, "there were 243."

"Two hundred forty-three is right," Casale agreed. "Do you want to hear the punch line?"

"Punch line?" the Saudi echoed.

"Right. The thing that makes a joke funny," Casale explained. "Are you ready?"

"I do not understand."

"Damn right, you don't. The punch line is, there should've been two hundred forty-*six*. Get it? Is that hilarious or what? Three people missed the flight."

Al-Rachid now looked confused. "This joke, you say—"

"A woman and two men," Casale interrupted. "What do you make of that?"

"Nothing. It is a common thing for travelers to miss a flight. Coincidence."

"Don't bet your camel on it, pal."

Al-Rachid bristled but held himself in check. Casale wished the Arab would explode, lash out at him. It would be pleasant to retaliate and beat him down, an outcome that Casale never doubted if the two of them were placed together in a cage where only one could walk away. But for the moment, they were allies, joined in common purpose.

And it made Casale sick.

"It makes no difference," al-Rachid informed him. "If we miss, we try again."

"No difference, you say? *No difference?*" Casale nearly struck the first blow then, from sheer frustration at al-Rachid's refusal to admit mistakes. "Let me explain the difference, and listen good. You killed nearly 250 people for no reason, which hits the airwaves as a tragedy. Police from here to Washington are on it like a swarm of flies on shit, and all you've got to say is 'try again'?"

The Arab's eyes flashed at Casale. "I will not be spoken to in such a manner, infidel. I took the action necessary to—"

"To what?" Casale cut him off. "Put all of us against a wall for army target practice? What you've done is put us all at risk *and* warn the targets. Spook them off to God knows where, while we're running for cover. That's some brilliant plan, Riyadh."

"Rachid," the Arab muttered.

"Whatever. Worse than all those other things you did, you went ahead and never told me! Do you understand *leaders* where you come from?"

"My leader is Kasim al-Bari," al-Rachid told him, not quite smiling. "He commands the Sword of Allah, which I serve."

"Not this time, buddy. Don Antonio Romano calls the shots on this one, as your sheikh or whatever the hell he is agreed. Down here, that means I call the shots, and no one ever mentioned bombing any goddamned plane to me."

"Blasphemer!"

"Listen up, and listen good. I don't like politics, and I don't give a shit about religion. You hate Jews for some reason. Means shit to me. What matters is the job and following my orders. You just fucked that up, and I'm not sure if we can fix it."

"You are rude and you exaggerate."

"Oh, yeah? Well, let me tell you this. You run around behind my back and pull this kind of shit again, I'll drop you in a hole myself. You hear me?"

"Rude, hysterical and with a high opinion of yourself."

Casale smiled, while he counted up to fifty in his head. "Last time I checked," he replied, "you had a dozen soldiers. I've got twenty-five, with more on tap. You want to mix it up and see who's standing when the smoke clears, we can go right now."

Al-Rachid was silent for a moment, seeming to consider it. At last, he said, "I have my orders, also. For the moment, they do not include eliminating you."

"In that case, I'll stop trembling," Casale said, sneering. "Get with your people and remind them that this isn't Baghdad or Beirut. I need to call the Don and tell him how your brilliant plan backfired."

"I, too, must use the telephone."

"We've only got the one line, Slick. You'll have to wait."

Al-Rachid glowered, then left and closed the study door behind him as Casale turned and reluctantly reached out for the telephone.

Manhattan, New York

ANTONIO ROMANO KNEW the prospect of a life in prison was a distinct possibility—if he didn't get the needle on the murder rap.

And when he broke it down, it was his own damned fault.

But it had seemed so easy! He was just the moneyman, taking a cut each time a dollar or a piece of merchandise passed through his hands. Weapons, vehicles, information, laundered cash—the usual.

And what was wrong with that?

Romano didn't care if his customers were labeled terrorists. A federal prosecutor had tried to hang the same tag on Romano once, after a little dust-up with some Teamsters who refused to do as they were told. Arabs and Jews were never going to be friends, and someone stood to make a killing from their conflict.

Why not me? Romano had decided.

Then, it blew up in his face. The FBI had bagged some Arabs out in California somewhere, setting up a score, and one of them rolled over on his buddies, telling what he knew about their deal with the Italians in New York. It wasn't much, a little teaser, but the G-men ran with it and somehow built a case that left Romano facing life inside a cage or death strapped on a gurney, with a needle in his arm.

Of course, they needed witnesses.

There weren't many to start with, and the best protection in the world won't keep a man alive if others are fanatically determined to destroy him. So it was that prosecutors in Romano's case discovered one fine morning that they had no case.

Until somebody thought about Gil Favor, played connect-the-dots and recognized the swindler as their one last chance to make Romano's charges stick.

He'd never been a quitter, so Romano naturally sent his best men south to do the job in San José. A spirit of cooperation led him to accept the offer of a backup team from his erstwhile partner, Kasim al-Bari, which gave him forty-odd men in the field.

Forty-something against one.

Those were the kind of odds Romano liked.

But once again, his plans were going sour right and left.

He could've ranted at Casale on the telephone, but what would be the point? Armand wasn't behind the stupid bombing, hadn't even known about it in advance, and it wasn't Romano's way to punish his best soldier for somebody else's failure.

He would be talking to al-Bari soon, and he was going to communicate his serious displeasure over the attack in San José. Not that the victims mattered to Romano, one way or another, but the fuckup may have jeopardized his future.

And he couldn't let that pass.

The problem with al-Bari was, he couldn't take constructive criticism.

Well, screw him.

If his people made Romano's situation worse by "helping," Don Antonio would make a point of settling their hash before the damage went from bad to terminal.

Unless it was too late already.

Shit, he thought, and reached out for the phone.

San José

ARMAND CASALE THOUGHT that he was clever, but Haroun al-Rachid was no fool himself. Rather than wait like a child or servant for permission to use the safehouse telephone, he found a room that would afford some privacy and palmed the sat phone that he carried with him everywhere, unknown to the Italian. It possessed a built-in scrambler that would let him speak frankly, without resort to tiresome codes.

Far off, somewhere in New York City, al-Rachid heard another telephone ring three times before a mellow tenor voice answered in Arabic.

"Kasim, it's me," al-Rachid began.

"Who else?" Kasim al-Bari replied.

"I have news," al-Rachid said.

"Let me guess. An airliner, perhaps, at the San José airport?"

Al-Rachid hesitated for only a heartbeat. "It's true. We were told that the target was flying this morning, with escorts. Romano's man was slow to act. I took the initiative."

"With what result, Haroun?" al-Bari asked.

"The device functioned perfectly," al-Rachid hedged.

"So I see, even now on my television screen. Now answer me."

"Casale claims three passengers were not aboard the flight," al-Rachid replied. "He leaps to the assumption that they are the same three whom we targeted. In fact—"

"Do you have *facts* for me, Haroun?"

"Sir, we don't know who missed the flight. Names from a manifest, but none belonging to the target."

"You assume that he would use his own passport and name? A wanted man? When was the last time you did that, Haroun?"

"It was the first thing that I thought of," al-Rachid answered. Even to himself, it sounded lame.

"Instinct is critical," al-Bari said. "But judgment always counts. Sometimes I think you've failed to learn the value of a surgical reaction. Narrow and precise. Eliminating this one man defends our cause without advancing it. Grand gestures are unnecessary—and, in fact, unwise."

"I understand, Kasim."

"But can you learn from your mistake?"

"Yes, sir. I can," al-Rachid assured his leader.

"I hope so, for all our sakes."

"I'll prove it to you!"

"How?"

Al-Rachid thought swiftly, blurting out, "I will identify the missing passengers and trace their reservations. Find out where they called from, if I can, then who they are. If one of them is Favor, I will track them down and finish it."

"With the Italians, yes?" al-Bari said. "For better or worse, in this instance we are comrades."

"As you say, Kasim. Comrades."

"So be it. Make me proud."

The line went dead. Al-Rachid switched off the phone, snapped it shut and returned it to his pocket. Stepping to the door, he opened it and used hand signals to attract his men.

They joined him without speaking, shooting sidelong glances toward the nearest open doorway, alert for any of Casale's gunmen passing by. Al-Rachid found it impossible to dignify the Sicilians as soldiers, since none had trained in the fine arts of war, and they apparently possessed no discipline beyond obedience to orders from their capo.

When the door had shut behind the last of al-Rachid's men, he spoke to them in muted, urgent tones. "The target lives," he told them bluntly, wasting no time on preliminaries. "While the bombing was flawless in concept and execution, still we have failed."

His men stood silent, grim-faced. They would not interrupt him, waiting instead until al-Rachid invited questions.

"Casale believes he can locate the target," he continued. "Whether his confidence is based on fact, I cannot say. We all are strangers here, not obvious to look at, but beyond that—" His dismissive gesture said it all. "We are compelled to wait and let Casale prove himself, or fail and finally admit to his employer that he cannot do the job he was assigned."

A dozen pairs of eyes were locked on al-Rachid's solemn face. He waited, stretched the moment until it almost seemed that they were trembling in unison, then said, "If the Italians fail, we must be ready with our own plan, ready to pursue the goal."

And still they waited, all united in their wish to serve, all equally uncertain as to how they should proceed in this, a foreign land where some of them spoke neither common language.

"First," al-Rachid suggested, "place yourselves inside the minds of those we hunt. Three runners, one of them a woman whose importance is unclear. The men are foreigners who stand out from the natives more than we do, at first glance, though one of them has lived in San José for several years and speaks the language. He has contacts, but they will not serve him now. Our enemies are hunted by both sides. It doesn't even matter which side finds them first, as long as they are silenced for eternity."

Eyes drilling into him, al-Rachid suppressed an urge to blink. "Your task now is to calculate what they will do, where they might go. Consider every possibility. Make lists. When you've exhausted every option, we will speak again. Questions?"

No hands went up.

"All right," al-Rachid said, offering his men a rare and arid smile. "Begin."

AMERICANS MADE Serafin Lazaro nervous. He had dealt with many in his time, all ages, different races and religions, but he'd found that all of them possessed a certain grating arrogance when dealing with Hispanic people south of the border. Each appeared to think that he was Teddy Roosevelt, wielding a big stick, giving orders, while the peons were expected to obey without complaint.

It pleased Lazaro, sometimes, to deflate those types. But while Armand Casale had the same infuriating attitude as countless others who had come before him, he was also an ambassador of men

Lazaro could not safely rile. Antonio Romano would remember if his front man suffered any disrespect, and while his present situation gave Romano the appearance of a badly wounded predator, the Mafia still had long arms.

"I may be able tó assist you, and am pleased to try," Lazaro told Casale, "but I make no promises. These people that you seek are likely to avoid my normal contacts."

"Hey," Casale said, "I understand that they're not smugglers. But they're moving a package from here to the States. I need to head them off in transit. Simple, right?"

"Well, hardly."

"What's the rub?" Casale asked. "A man with your connections, always in the know and on the go, moving whatever and *who*ever needs to move, you've gotta have this whole place wired. Or am I wrong?"

"You are correct," Lazaro said, long years of practice granting him the strength to curb his temper. "On the other hand, you were correct as well in saying that the people whom you seek are not smugglers. In fact, we have no reason to believe that they are criminals at all."

"Hold on. They waste eight of my men, then split, and you say they're not criminals? I'm guessing there's some cops in San José who'd disagree with you."

"Of course," Lazaro stated, "they have broken local laws, including some quite serious. But we must face the possibility that two of them, the escorts, may be agents of your government."

"My government is full of criminals," Casale said. "Trust me."

"I understand. But these, perhaps, rely on some official aid in their pursuits outside of the United States."

"You mean, like spies and shit?"

"A possibility to be considered."

"I considered it already," Casale said. "I've got two men camped out at the embassy. They tell me Favor hasn't shown his face within two blocks. I've got a couple guys inside the state police who say the hunt is on for Favor and his pals, despite the bribes he's paid for coverage the past few years. You've got no extradition treaty with the States, no U.S. military bases where these pricks could hide him, waiting for black helicopters or whatever. Am I missing something here?"

"Perhaps not," Lazaro replied. "But, then again…"

Lazaro was uncomfortable in Casale's safehouse, even with his car and three armed men outside. It was the kind of situation where his first mistake could be his last.

"Come on, for Christ's sake. Spit it out," Casale said.

"It is well-known—to your employers, certainly—that U.S. agents operate in countries where no embassies exist. In point of fact, they are more likely to be found in such places, seeking whatever crumbs of information may be found. The CIA, the NSA, even your FBI—"

"It's not *my* fucking FBI," Casale interrupted him.

"In any case, we must accept that agents are abroad in San José. Whole networks may exist, of which I'm unaware."

"That's sloppy work," Casale said.

Lazaro felt the angry color rising in his cheeks. He hoped his dark complexion covered it. "I am a businessman," he said. "I deal in various commodities—"

"Cocaine and heroin," Casale interrupted. "Weapons, women, wetbacks. I was told you also deal in information."

"You were told correctly."

"So, inform me."

"It may take some time, you realize."

"The one thing I don't have. Will money help?"

Lazaro smiled. "Señor Casale, money *always* helps."

New York City

"WE COULD BE IN the shit." Antonio Romano spoke around a fat cigar tucked in the corner of his mouth. "I asked you over here to see what we can do about it."

Romano's call had not surprised Kasim al-Bari, but it did irritate him on several levels. First, he was not a dog to be summoned to fetch a newspaper or pair of slippers. Second, any meeting with Romano vastly increased al-Bari's personal risks—of unmasking, disgrace, deportation. Finally, al-Bari had the sense that Romano would soon be a burden instead of an asset.

If the witness lived to testify…

Romano's second in command, John Fabrizio, sat watching al-Bari as if he expected the Saudi to produce a magic lamp and grant Romano powers to make all his problems disappear.

I'm not Aladdin, al-Bari thought. He suppressed an urge to smile, knowing that it would be a critical mistake.

"I share your sense of urgency," al-Bari said, "and I am open to suggestions."

"*Open* to suggestions?" Leaning forward through a cloud of acrid smoke, Romano told him, "I was hoping you might *make* a few goddamned suggestions, since your people down in Costa Rica screwed the pooch."

"Excuse me?" Other than the obvious insult suggesting bestiality, al-Bari found Romano's comment utterly incomprehensible.

"They fucked up, get it?" Anger strained the mafioso's voice. "They're s'posed to help me cap one guy and save our asses. Yours *and* mine. Instead, they kill two-hundred-something, get the cops down there all hopping mad and let the target skate. That's what I mean."

"The plan was poorly executed, I agree."

"You said a mouthful there, Kasim." Romano sat back in his chair, the pose of relaxation failing to dilute the menace in his attitude. "In fact, I'd say the plan was doomed *before* your people started executing it."

"And if this bookkeeper had been aboard the plane, what would you say?" al-Bari asked.

"Unless you've got a way to turn back time, it makes no difference," Romano said. "I'm in shit up to my neck, and you're right in there with me. Just because they haven't put your name on an indictment yet, don't think you're in the clear."

"I'm confident the situation can be rectified," al-Bari said. "Your syndicate—"

"My *Family*," Romano pointedly corrected him.

"Your *Family* must have connections in the area, persons who help transport your merchandise from South America to the United States.

Logic dictates that they will know the best routes of evasion and escape. Mount round-the-clock surveillance on those routes, and—"

"Jesus Christ!" Romano wore a look of mock amazement as he turned to face Fabrizio. "I never thought of that! Go out and *look* for them? It's brilliant!"

"You are pleased to joke at my expense," al-Bari said.

"That's where you're wrong, Kasim. Nothing that's happened in the past few days has pleased me. You can take my word on that."

"What would you have me do?" the Saudi asked. "I've already spoken to the leader of my team in San José. He understands the problem fully and regrets the failure of his plan, however well-conceived it may have been. My soldiers are at your disposal, Don Romano. I can do no more."

"Maybe you can."

"Meaning?"

"Meaning," Romano said, "that if you've got some kind of goofy shit lined up before this trouble gets resolved and the indictments are dismissed, forget about it. I've got heat enough—without any new reports of poison gas on subways, airplanes crashing into buildings, anything like that. If you've got something cooking, take it off the burner. Then turn off the stove."

Kasim al-Bari imagined how good it would feel to slash this infidel's throat and watch him drown in his own stinking blood. The sheer presumption of him, dictating a schedule to the Sword of Allah!

Then again, al-Bari realized that if he argued with Romano there, in the mobster's own den, he might sign his own death warrant.

"You need have no concern," he told Romano, smiling thinly. "I want nothing more than peace."

And I will have it, al Bari thought, when my enemies are dead and rotting in their graves.

7

Hal Brognola tensed when the gray phone on his desk rang. That was his hotline, bypassing the Justice switchboard, and its number was known to fewer than two dozen people.

Brognola lifted the receiver. "Hello."

"It's me," the deep, familiar voice announced.

Brognola felt relief wash over him. "It's good to hear from you," he said.

"I guess you've heard about the incident," Bolan said, spare with details even on the scrambled line.

"It was a big deal on the tube for about an hour," Brognola told him. "That was—what, four hours ago?"

"I know. Sorry I couldn't reach you sooner, but it's been a zoo down here."

"I can imagine," Brognola replied. He understood the chaos that ensued when disaster struck. "I guess you won't be flying out."

"Not out of San José, at least," Bolan agreed. "The airport should be up and running soon, but with the new, enhanced security, we couldn't risk it."

"What's Plan B?" Brognola asked, knowing that Bolan had to have called for help.

"We have new wheels," Bolan said, "and our paperwork is still intact, so driving is an option, but we'll have to deal with checkpoints all the way. The other way's a private charter flight, but I'm not sure about the local pilots."

"What about a special pickup? I can get in touch with Jack and see if he's available."

This time, it was his old friend's turn to sound relieved, though Bolan masked it well. "I figured he'd be on a job," Bolan replied.

"He is," the big Fed said, "but nothing life-or-death. I'll make a call."

"Appreciate it," Bolan said, then let the moment go. "We're heading north along the main route, toward the border, just in case he doesn't make it for whatever reason."

"You know Jack," Brognola said. "When he gets something in his head, there's just no stopping him."

"Okay," Bolan said. "Give him my number when you get a chance, and he can call me when he's ready. We'll work something out."

"Will do," Brognola said. "Meanwhile, if you need anything…"

"We're good," Bolan replied.

"Right. So long, then."

Bolan killed the link, and Brognola reached out to cradle the receiver.

Heading north along the main route.

That could only mean they were driving along the Pan-American Highway, northbound from San José toward Nicaragua and whatever lay beyond its border.

If they got that far.

Bolan had spoken of checkpoints, referring to the various border crossings where guards could search approaching vehicles on a whim, dealing with the occupants more or less as they saw fit.

One look in Bolan's trunk or duffel bag, wherever he was carrying his military hardware on this road trip, and the journey would be over. Bolan wouldn't fight arrest, had pledged that he would never kill a good cop regardless of the circumstances, so a stop-and-search meant jail.

And jail meant death.

Tony Romano's goons were already out for Gil Favor, willing to kill anybody who got in their way. The San José airport bombing proved that, and mere prison walls would not protect Favor or his escorts. Not in a country where everything and everyone had a price tag attached.

The pickup was critical, which raised a whole new set of

problems for Brognola. He would have to deal with all of them before help reached his oldest living friend.

Get started, then, he thought, and reached out once more for the telephone.

Phoenix, Arizona

THE SAT PHONE'S SOFT vibration startled Jack Grimaldi. He had turned off the ringer at breakfast, afraid of spooking his two charter passengers. Still, they were both getting restless, alternately eyeballing the vast desert below and checking their gold watches.

"How much longer?" asked the fat one, Milton Jaffe. He was belted into the copilot's seat of the Gulfstream American GA7 Cougar, meaty calves and wingtip shoes clamped tight around a briefcase that held two million dollars in hundred-dollar bills.

Two hundred bundles, that would be, one hundred bills per bundle. Sweet.

Behind Grimaldi, Jaffe's partner peered through one of the Gulfstream's small windows, watching their shadow skim over the wasteland below. Cliff Barnes, he called himself. Six inches taller than his sidekick, and still some twenty pounds lighter by Grimaldi's estimate.

Not counting the weight of the gun he was packing.

Their destination was a ranch outside of Tucson, sixty miles or so. For a fraction of the price Grimaldi charged, they could've driven out from town, less than an hour on the road at posted speeds, then done their business and driven back in time for dinner at a stylish restaurant. But Jaffe was afraid of trouble on the highway—cops, hijackers, whatever—and he liked the fact that flying shaved forty minutes off his travel time, each way.

He couldn't know that trouble wasn't lurking on the two-lane desert road below. It was already waiting for him at the ranch.

And it was riding in the pilot's seat.

Jaffe and Barnes were drug smugglers. Grimaldi had encountered them by accident and volunteered to help put them away. Twenty miles ahead of him, a team including federal, state and county officers was waiting for the Gulfstream to touch down, depositing the moneymen. An undercover agent would be waiting with another suitcase, this one filled with parcels borrowed from a DEA evidence locker, and once the cash changed hands it would be handcuff time.

Then Grimaldi could answer his phone.

"Vista Ranch coming up," he announced.

"It's about freaking time," Barnes replied. He was just short of airsick, and not hiding it well.

"Buckle up if you haven't already," Grimaldi advised. "I'll begin the approach."

He ran the mental checklist, lowering the landing gear and lining up on the asphalt-paved runway, which shimmered with heat waves. The ranch seemed deserted, no squad cars or other suspicious vehicles evident from his bird's-eye view. Grimaldi wondered whether they were in the barn, or if they had been ferried back to town as part of the illusion.

Anything, he guessed, to make the trap secure.

Jaffe glanced over his shoulder, grinning and flashing a thumbs-up at Barnes. The tall man, for his part, just grunted and glared.

The landing went well. One bounce, then they settled and taxied. Grimaldi could feel his passengers relax, but there was still anticipation in their attitude. Drug buys went south nearly as often as they came together smoothly. Drugs and cash were stolen. People died.

Grimaldi felt his phone vibrate again, insistently, against his ribs. Hang on, he thought, and concentrated on the last few yards before he nosed the Gulfstream up to the barn. It was the spot that he'd been told to use, marked with a black X on aerial photos.

We're here, folks, Grimaldi thought. Come and get it.

Grimaldi killed the engines, unbuckled his harness and moved toward the exit hatch. He unlatched and opened it, lowered the folding steps and stood aside to let his passengers deplane.

"Not bad," Jaffe said as he stepped into the doorway. From the barn, a figure was approaching, one hand raised in greeting. "Here's the man. Come on, Cliff."

"Right behind you," Barnes replied. He stood hunched over in the Gulfstream's passenger compartment, one hand tucked inside his windbreaker, clutching his gun.

Jaffe descended, hand outstretched to shake the vendor's while Grimaldi watched him through the open hatch. Barnes hesitated, then began to follow his companion—just as members of a wait-ing SWAT team suddenly erupted from the barn and farmhouse, racing to surround the aircraft in their jet-black uniforms and body armor, automatic weapons leveled, hard eyes steady under Kevlar helmets.

Jaffe dropped his bag and raised both hands before the raiders had a chance to warn him. Barnes, by contrast, turned and rushed back up the airplane's folding steps, drawing his pistol as he came.

"Screw this!" he snapped. "We're getting out of here!"

Grimaldi nailed him with a solid right between the eyes, putting his weight behind it. Barnes tumbled into Jaffe and they both col-lapsed in a heap, ringed by the uniforms and guns.

Just as Grimaldi's sat phone vibrated again.

This time, he fished it from his pocket, read the number on display and smiled. He put it to his ear and told Brognola, "Speak to me."

Pan-American Highway, Costa Rica

THEIR NEW RIDE WAS a year-old SUV, appropriated from a shopping mall on the northern outskirts of San José. Bolan had filled its tank with gasoline at a last-chance service station on his way out of town, rolling northward toward Alajuela.

It was a fifteen-mile drive from the nation's capital, mountain roads all the way, through Costa Rica's Cordillera Central. If Bolan had been sightseeing, he might've stopped for snapshots of the four volcanoes that towered between San José and Alajuela—Barva, Irazú, Poás and Turrialba. As it was, he kept his full attention on the road, with frequent glances at his rearview mirror to check for a tail.

Blanca Herrera was riding shotgun, literally, with their bags of weapons at her feet. Gil Favor had the backseat to himself, child-safety locks engaged on the back doors to counter any sudden urge that might compel him to bail out and break his neck.

After a brief and desultory argument, Favor had given up and lapsed into depressive silence. He stared out the windows, studying the countryside as they gained altitude, but keeping any ideas or fears to himself.

Just as well, Bolan thought. He'd known Favor for only fourteen hours, give or take, and he was already sick of the fugitive's nagging. Until the airliner exploded, Favor had seemed certain that he could elude Romano's hunters on his own. Now it appeared that he had given up on life itself.

"Will we stop in Alajuela?" Herrera asked him.

"Not unless somebody needs a bathroom break," Bolan replied. Reviewing the map in his head, Bolan added, "We've got plenty of stops on the way. Barranca's only forty-four miles farther on, then another sixty to Liberia. Beyond Liberia, it's forty-five miles to the border."

"And we cross there?"

"That's the plan," he said. "Our lift will take at least five hours reaching us, and that's if he's already airborne. Call it six or seven, if we figure that he had to make arrangements for the unexpected hop. That means we either cross today or find someplace to spend the night and hope no one is looking for us."

"They'll be looking," Favor muttered from the backseat.

"But will they look outside of San José?" Herrera asked. Bolan noticed that she spoke to him, not Favor.

"They'll check the city first," Bolan said, "but they may not stop there. If they're smart, they will have figured out that I'm American, and that I don't want Favor dead. That tells them that he's needed in the States, most likely for Romano's trial. That means I wouldn't take him south, toward Panama, and make things even worse. If they've got San José sewed up—the airport, buses, trains—it means we've gone to ground, or else I'm driving him."

"Searching the city will take time," Herrera observed.

Nodding agreement, Bolan added, "But they won't *just* search the city if they're smart."

"They're smart, all right," Favor said, sounding glum.

Bolan ignored him, telling Herrera, "Whoever's in charge will know that every hour they spend scouring San José helps us, if we're not there. If I was running it, and I had men to spare, I'd keep a sharp eye on the highways headed north."

"Well, they can't catch us now," Herrera said, settling back into her seat.

Behind her, Favor snorted. "Did you ever hear of helicopters, sweetheart? How about an airplane? Jesus, they could be waiting for us now, in any of those towns you named. Maybe in *all* of them."

"He's right," Bolan agreed. "It's possible. Not definite, but definitely possible."

"And if they *are* there, then what?" she inquired.

"In that case," Bolan said, "we fight."

"WE FIGHT," Gil Favor muttered to himself, not loud enough for anyone to hear. "And who the hell is *we?*"

Not him, for sure. He couldn't picture either of his escorts handing him a weapon, even in the heat of battle when their lives were riding on the line. They wouldn't trust him, and with reason. Favor was adept at looking out for number one and letting everybody else do likewise.

Somehow, so far, he'd always managed to come out on top—or close enough, at least, that he had decent money in his pocket.

Until this time.

This time he had no one to bail him out but the unlikely couple riding with him in the stolen SUV. His crooked cops had failed him, hadn't tipped him that a hit team was in town and looking for him. Favor could forgive the politicians, since they might not be informed that someone from the U.S. government was coming to abduct him, but the rest of them?

Forget it.

They were cut off, as of now, cold turkey. Let Romano pay for all their toys, lovers and luxuries, if he was so inclined. A deal like that, Favor supposed the buyer never really got his money's worth.

Now, here he was with Bonnie and Clyde, cruising toward almost certain death in the middle of the Costa Rican mountains.

Strangely, although he knew his hours might be numbered, Favor wasn't in a panic. That surprised him. Fleeting macho fantasies aside, he'd always thought that when it came down to the wire, he'd lose it absolutely and disgrace himself.

But no.

He wasn't calm, exactly, but his hands weren't trembling, and he didn't feel incessant longing for a toilet. Maybe when the moment came, and he was looking down a gun barrel, then the gravity of his situation would finally hit home. But for the moment, he was getting by.

Amazing.

"Do we have a plan?" he asked his escorts, turning from the mountain vista outside his window to study the backs of their heads. "I only ask because…well, you know…I appear to have some interest in the outcome."

"Job one," Bolan said, "is keeping you alive until the handoff in New York."

"That's nice to hear," Favor said. "But I have to tell you, I was hoping for a few more details."

"Sorry. Your ex-friends forgot to let me see their playbook."

"We can pretty well assume they'll try to stop the car and kill me, right? Which means they'll kill the two of you, as well."

"Broad strokes, I'd say you've got it down," Bolan said.

"And what I'm asking you is how you plan to stop them," Favor prodded him.

"You're talking hypothetically," Bolan answered, "but that's all a waste of time and energy. Response to aerial attack is different from a car chase, which is different from dealing with a sniper."

"Obviously," Favor countered, feeling irritated now. "But for my peace of mind, such as it is, I'd like to know if you're up to the job."

"We haven't lost you yet," the Executioner told him, almost cheerfully.

"That's it? You haven't lost me *yet?*"

"Get over it," Bolan answered. "You want guarantees, I'll give you one. We'll do our best to keep you breathing. That's the deal. You think Romano has a better offer for you, I can drop you off right here and let you take your chances."

Favor didn't call the empty bluff. He wasn't getting out on some mountain road in the middle of nowhere, assuming his escorts would let him—and that was a crock in itself. They hadn't come this far, fought this hard and risked so much, to simply boot his ass out of the car.

They were in it for the long haul, all the way back to Manhattan or wherever Romano was scheduled for trial. Personally, Favor didn't think he'd ever see the inside of that courtroom, but he wasn't giving up without a struggle. When the bastards came to kill him, he would make them work for it.

"We fight," the driver had proclaimed a moment earlier.

Favor decided he could live with that.

Alajuela

TWO MILES BEFORE they reached the town, Blanca Herrera started seeing villagers along both shoulders of the mountain highway, slowly moving toward or from the settlement on which they relied for most of their supplies.

Some of the peasants halted in their plodding progress, tracked the SUV with weary eyes, while others seemed to let it pass without a glance. That wasn't true, however, Herrera realized. These people stayed alive by seeing *everything* around them and reacting in a manner that would minimize risk to themselves. They always knew when strangers came and went, but getting information from them on the subject would be difficult, if not impossible.

No matter, she decided, since they had no plans to stop in Alajuela. If an ambush waited for them, they would simply have to deal with it, as Cooper said.

The bags of weapons at her feet gave her added confidence. Next time that they ran into trouble, if there was a next time, she would not have to rely entirely on her pistol and its one spare magazine. Next time, she would be in the middle of the action, fighting for their fugitive at Cooper's side.

The prospect frightened and excited her.

As Alajuela came within their view, she glanced across and saw that they had ample fuel to reach the border without stopping. If the choice was hers, she'd recommend another stop before that point, perhaps when they were in Barranca, but she left that choice to Cooper.

"You mentioned stopping for a bathroom break," Favor said from the rear.

"No dice," Cooper said with a quick glance toward the rearview mirror. "See the empty water jug back there? That's what it's for."

"Jesus. I'd like a little privacy, you know? A little dignity."

"I gave you dignity back at the airport," Bolan told him. "Now, you've got the jug."

"Forget it. I can wait."

"Your call. We promise not to peek, if you change your mind."

Despite that promise, Herrera glanced back at their prisoner and found him peering through the tinted window on his left, then shifting to his right, repeating the inspection of Alajuela's main street. She wondered what Favor was looking for, then understood that he was worried, watching out for gunmen bent on killing him.

"They don't know where you are," she said.

"Which means they'll keep on looking," he replied. "You think this car has been reported stolen yet?"

"It's probable," Cooper said, "but there's nothing to connect us with it. San José must have a hundred auto thefts per day."

"Closer to double that," Herrera said. "It's a minor scandal. Newspapers are always calling for new legislation, harsher punishment for car thieves. It's the same with drugs and burglaries."

"Okay, two hundred stolen cars today," Bolan replied. "Assume Romano has his own eyes on the force—"

"A safe assumption," Favor interjected. "I do. Or, I did."

"That means they have to look at all two hundred thefts and guess which vehicle we took, after they check the rental agencies and retail dealerships. If that's their only angle of attack, you could be safe at home while they're still sorting files."

"This was my home," Favor retorted.

"No. This was your hideout. There's a difference," Cooper said.

"Not if your bank accounts are fat enough."

"How does it feel to be so wealthy?" Herrera asked.

That won a smile from Favor, tinged with bitter irony. "You grow accustomed to it," he replied. "Like being poor, only without the hunger, the disease, the stinking dead-end job with lousy pay. You ought to try it sometime."

"That's not likely," she reminded him.

"It could be."

Cooper glared at Favor in the rearview, and their passenger responded with a shrug. "Hey, I'm just saying. Right? The offer's out there, if you change your minds."

"We won't," Cooper assured him.

"No, we won't," Herrera echoed the tall American.

She settled back, hands resting on her knees, above the open bags of weapons, as they rolled through town, waiting for enemies she'd never seen before to spring their trap and try to end her life.

8

San José

Pablo Morales didn't understand why he was looking for the company that owned a rental car, but it was not his place to question orders. He had received a license number for the vehicle in question, and he understood that Serafin Lazaro wished to know its source.

What more was there to know?

The search made a change for Morales from his normal duties, which included torturing and killing those who had displeased Señor Lazaro in some way. It seemed unlikely that his special talent for inflicting pain would be required for his present assignment, but the very fact of his selection told Morales that the matter was important.

He'd begun with the rental agencies located at San José's airport. They clustered together near the cavernous baggage-claim area, making it simple for new arrivals to obtain ground transportation. Five agencies served the airport, and Morales visited each one in turn, flashing a badge that he had taken from the body of a foolish and corrupt policeman who had trifled with Señor Lazaro and who'd lived—albeit briefly—to regret his folly.

At each rental counter Morales followed the same procedure. A flash of his badge, and the glowering question without explanation. Each time, the attendant typed commands into a computer, then informed him that there was no record of the vehicle in question.

Strange.

After his fifth consecutive defeat, Morales paused to consider his next step. It would have helped to know whom he was looking for, but going back to Señor Lazaro for more information was out of the question. Instead, he found a small, uncomfortable bench, sat down and tried to puzzle through the problem.

He imagined a visitor new to the city and in need of a car. The person had either not come by air, or else he had chosen to bypass all the airport rental agencies. The reason? Obviously, to obscure his trail.

Which meant the man—or woman, perhaps—had expected to be hunted.

If the hunted one had flown to San José yet chosen a rental agency located somewhere other than the airport, then preliminary transportation was required. That meant a taxi, bus or private vehicle—in which case, Morales was hunting not one man, but two. Maybe more.

Yet, if they had a car, why rent another one?

Again, to hide the trail.

Morales rose and moved along the concourse to the nearest public telephone. Consulting its directory, he found a list of auto rental agencies whose offices were scattered throughout the city. Three of them were branches of the airport agencies, which raised a question in his mind. The other nine were smaller independent firms that were unable to afford an office at the airport.

He would have to check them all.

Before returning to his own car in the airport's short-term parking lot, Morales retraced his steps to the car-rental booths. The attendants all remembered him and answered his new question with alacrity. Two solemnly assured him that their database included all vehicles held and rented by their companies in San José. The third regretted to inform him that they could not access records for the satellite facility, which might indeed maintain the vehicle he sought.

Eliminating two stops from his mental list, Morales walked back through the terminal to reach the exit nearest the garage. He did not spare a glance for the police who circulated through the concourse in their two-man teams. They had no reason to accost him, were too busy or too negligent to spot the pistol holstered underneath his roomy sport coat.

If they found him with the dead detective's badge, of course, there would be hell to pay. A rough interrogation to begin with, which Morales knew he could withstand. Later, if they did not believe his tale of purchasing the badge from someone on the street whom he could not identify, he might be charged. If there was evidence of murder, he would be imprisoned for a minimum of sixteen years.

But none of that would happen. Long before the case could go to trial, Señor Lazaro would exert his influence, the evidence would be misplaced and Pablo Morales would be free again to serve his master.

As he always had, and always would.

Three of the rental agencies he had to check were situated near San José's main bus depots, two on Second Avenue, the third ten blocks farther south. He would check those three first, then move on to the others if need be, connecting the dots and plotting his course as he drove.

Morales wondered what the man or men he hunted had done to anger Señor Lazaro. It could be anything, and now he hoped that if he found the scum—or even if someone else did—the boss might let him mete out punishment.

Pablo Morales lived to serve.

Airborne over Chihuahua, Mexico

JACK GRIMALDI HAD SPENT a tense half hour answering questions in Tucson, talking to the DEA and state police alike, then learned that the Learjet 23 aircraft he wanted for his flight to Costa Rica wasn't instantly available. He had waited through the worst part of a fretful hour for it to be fueled and fully serviced, then clearance for his takeoff took another fifteen minutes, by which time he was fuming silently, white-knuckling the controls.

Now he was airborne, and it seemed to be taking forever, even at the Learjet's standard cruising speed of 481 miles per hour. The flight from Tucson to San José would consume five hours and change, dead time for Grimaldi when anything could happen to his good friend on the ground.

Stony Man was handling arrangements at the other end, making acquisitions to Grimaldi's specifications. He'd have to trust the Farm on that part and hope they got it right, to avoid wasting more precious time on arrival.

When he had the Lear on automatic pilot, bound for Yucatán and his refueling stop, Grimaldi tried the sat phone. Brognola had supplied the number, which was changed at monthly intervals for reasons of security.

He tapped the number out from memory, no saving it on speed-dial, and it rang once, somewhere far away, before the strong, familiar voice responded.

"Hey," Grimaldi said. "I understand you need a lift."

"It wouldn't hurt," Bolan replied.

"I'm about four hours north of San José. Was there a pickup point you had in mind?" Grimaldi asked.

"We're on the road and making decent time," Bolan explained. "About three hours from the border, at our present speed. I guess it means more trouble if we cross before you get here."

"I've got a chopper waiting on the ground in San José," Grimaldi replied. "I'm not sure whether I can get one in Managua, so I'd have to fly across the border. That's no sweat, as far as I'm concerned, but it could amplify your problems if we're spotted."

"Roger that," Bolan said. "We can likely find someplace to stop and kill an hour on the highway. Let me have a quick word with my navigator on that pickup point."

"I'm standing by," Grimaldi said.

Dead silence filled his ear for ninety seconds, then Bolan's voice returned. "Okay," the warrior said, "we've got a place up near the border that's supposed to be a ghost town. Agua Caliente. You should have no problem setting down a chopper."

"Can you give me the coordinates?"

After a brief delay, Bolan rattled off a set of GPS coordinates. Grimaldi memorized them on the spot and said, "Okay, we're good. I ought to see you there at 2200 hours, give or take."

"Sounds good," Bolan replied. "Stay frosty, eh?"

"My middle name," Grimaldi said, and broke the link.

Ten o'clock would be cutting it close, Grimaldi thought, with a four-hour flight still ahead of him, plus the refueling stop in Yucatán and whatever time it took for him to claim his chopper in San José, then pilot it north to the chosen LZ.

A ghost town, for God's sake.

Agua Caliente. *Hot water.*

He smiled and told the Learjet's instrument array, "Hot water, here I come."

Continental Divide, Colombia

"HE'S COMING, THEN? Your friend?" Herrera inquired.

"He'll be there," Bolan answered, "but the timing is a problem."

Briefly, he explained the need to stop somewhere along their route and kill an hour, giving Grimaldi a chance to land in San José and switch aircraft before they crossed the border into Nicaragua.

"It's fifty-fifty," he concluded, "whether we pull over and stand down, or drive on into Agua Caliente and wait there. We have risk factors either way."

"Depending on who follows us," she said.

"And how they do it," Bolan added. "If they're still making the rounds in San José, we ought to be all right. If they spread out, we may have someone after us already. Or they could be waiting up ahead."

"So soon?" Her voice was taut.

"Precautionary measures," Bolan said. "Say that Romano's people want to hedge their bets. It won't cost much to fly a team of shooters north and pick a spot along the highway, wait to head us off."

"We're trapped, then," Herrera said.

"Not necessarily. They have to spot us first, and even then, it doesn't mean we're in the bag."

"But it looks bad, yes?" she asked a moment later.

"I've been in tighter spots," Bolan answered honestly.

"So, you believe we'll be all right?"

"I'm not a fortune-teller, Blanca, but we've got a fighting chance. And with the airlift…"

"If he finds us. If he's not too late."

"Don't *if* yourself to death on this thing. Take each moment as it comes."

"Is there a twelve-step program?" she asked Bolan, teasing.

"No. It's one step at a time."

The dashboard oil light winked at Bolan, just a glint of red. He watched it blink twice more, before it stayed on, cherry-bright. He checked the engine-heat gauge, saw no worrisome increase in temperature, but knew he had to take the warning seriously.

"Looks like we'll be stopping in Barranca, after all," he said.

"What's wrong?" Herrera asked.

Bolan pointed at the indicator light and said, "With any luck, we just need oil. If it's the line or something else, we have a problem."

"More than one," Herrera said, with a glance toward the backseat. At the same time, she nudged one of the duffels with her foot. The weapons shifted, clanking softly.

"If it's a low oil level, we won't have to leave the car," Bolan replied. "Even repairs don't mean they'll get to search our bags. Not if we're sharp."

Herrera caught Bolan's eye, pointed again to the backseat and cocked an eyebrow, questioning. Bolan responded with a shrug and said, "We stay alert. That's all."

They were roughly halfway between Alajuela and Barranca, twenty-odd miles to go before they could find a mechanic to look at the car. Bolan already knew he couldn't let a stranger drive the hot-wired vehicle. A fool could see that there was no ignition key, a sure sign that the SUV was stolen.

Not a problem, he decided. If he had to put it on the rack, Bolan would drive the car himself, watch over it while the repairs were made, then take the wheel to back it out of the garage.

Simple.

Herrera could help him watch Gil Favor at the same time, making sure that their reluctant passenger didn't try to escape a second time. The sedative syringe was still available, if Favor gave them any trouble, but he couldn't very well inject their captive in front of an audience of witnesses.

"No worries, eh?" Herrera said.

Bolan thought she sounded as if she was trying to convince herself.

"No worries, right," he said.

And hoped that it was true.

San José

"YOU FOUND THE RENTAL agency?" Armand Casale asked.

"Indeed." The smile on Serafin Lazaro's face was tentative, subdued.

"So, tell me," Casale prompted.

"It is near the depot where the bus from Puntarenas stops. An independent business, with no connection to the larger firms."

"They verified the rental?"

"Yes. But I'm afraid it helps us very little."

"Spill it anyway."

Lazaro shrugged. "Their records show the car was rented to a North American named Andrew Hardy. I have here a photocopy of the driver's license he presented to the clerk."

Lazaro took the folded paper from an inside pocket of his coat and gave it to Casale. Casale opened it, blinked at the copy of a driver's license with its small, generic photograph of an unsmiling face.

"I never saw this guy before," he said. "But Andy Hardy? Who's he kidding?"

"I'm afraid I do not understand," Lazaro said.

"You had to be there, pal. Old movies. Mickey Rooney? Never mind. To hell with it. The name's a phony, 'kay?"

"I see."

"What else?" Casale demanded.

"Very little, I'm afraid. The man paid with a credit card, which was accepted by the firm's validation network. He waived insurance on the vehicle. That's all."

"That's all?" Casale rose to pace the room. "Don't tell me that. There must be something else. I saw that he had someone with him in the car, besides Gil Favor. Did you ask the clerk if he had company?"

"I did. They are required to ask if someone other than the renter will be driving. His reply was negative. The clerk saw no one with him, no one waiting in the parking lot or on the street."

"Slick bastard!"

Casale fumed at meeting yet another roadblock. He was on a deadline, damn it. Every minute counted, and he felt them slipping through his fingers, lost forever while his target got away.

Not yet.

"Okay," he said. "What else?"

"Having secured a copy of the driver's license, my man revisited the other rental agencies. Regrettably, none had a record of your Mr. Hardy."

"Christ! He'd likely use another name!"

"There was the photograph, as well. None of the other clerks remember him."

"Okay. The hot cars, then."

Lazaro frowned. "As you requested, I made inquiries with the police, concerning stolen vehicles."

"And?"

"During the past twenty-four hours, 146 auto thefts were reported in San José. My source estimates that more will be reported in the morning, cars the owners don't miss overnight."

"Shit! A hundred fifty cars or more? What about witnesses? Did anything stand out?"

"Unfortunately, no. Some of the vehicles were taken by force—how you say it, carjacked?"

"That's how we say it," Casale confirmed.

"In those cases, police have descriptions. Even one holdup on videotape, from security cameras outside a mall. The carjackers are young, native boys, nearly all from street gangs. There is no Andrew Hardy among them."

"Goddamn it! People don't evaporate like this! They must be somewhere!"

"You're correct, of course," Lazaro said. "My men are scouring the city as we speak. Hotels and boardinghouses, bus depots, the taxi companies. If need be, we can try the restaurants."

"Screw that," Casale snapped. "I don't care where they ate, unless we catch them at the table. What I need is something else besides this bullshit name. Somebody saw this prick. Somebody saw his sidekick, too."

"You saw them," Lazaro said.

"Doesn't count," Casale answered bitterly. "Guy had his high beams in my face. Two shapes inside the car were all I saw, before…"

He didn't want to think about the riverfront fiasco or what it had cost him, either in troops or damage to his nerve.

The phone rang on Casale's desk. He snatched it up and barked, "Yeah, what?"

A small voice asked for Serafin Lazaro. Scowling, Casale said, "For you," and passed the receiver across his desk.

Lazaro said, *"Sí"* into the mouthpiece, then listened for the best part of a minute, nodding. He finished with a simple *"Gracias"* and reached across to cradle the receiver.

"There is hope," he said. "One of my spotters in Barranca says two gringos and a woman stopped to have their car checked at the town's garage. It needed oil. They purchased some, and then went on their way."

"Where in hell's Barranca?"

"North," Lazaro said. "Toward Nicaragua."

"Tourists, do you think?"

Lazaro shrugged. "I could arrange to fax the Hardy license, if you wish. My man can speak to the mechanics."

"Do that," Casale answered. "Do it now."

"ANOTHER HOUR WASTED, but at least we got a hit," Casale said.

Haroun al-Rachid watched the Sicilian pacing, felt the anger radiating from him. He believed that Casale was nearing the point that Americans liked to call a meltdown.

It should be amusing to watch.

"The same man?" he inquired, nonchalant.

"So they claim. Now we need to get up there."

"Up *where?*" al-Rachid asked.

"To Barranca. Some jerk-water town between here and the border. That's where they were spotted, for Christ's sake. Try to stay with me on this."

Al-Rachid swallowed the first retort that came to mind, instead replying with a question. "You are following this lead yourself?"

"Damned right, I am. We don't know if this bastard's stopping for the night or moving on, but I can be there in an hour with the chopper, give or take. Lazaro's guys are checking out the town, hotels and shit like that, but I need in on this."

"I see."

"Do you? I dropped the ball with Favor and his playmates on the first pass. Lost some men and took a bath myself, while they ran off to God knows where. My reputation's riding on the line with this—and so is yours."

"You wish me to accompany you?" he asked.

"Hey, that's your call," Casale answered. "All I'm saying is, if I'd blown up a couple hundred people and missed the guy I was trying for, I might want to wipe that slate clean, if you follow my drift."

Al-Rachid understood. The Sicilian made sense, despite his overwrought condition, but al-Rachid still wondered if Casale might be putting too much faith in a hasty report from the field.

"And if Lazaro's man is wrong," he said, "then what?"

"He made the photo, pal. Jesus!"

The Saudi leaned forward for another look at Casale's photocopy of an American driver's license. He studied the small, grainy likeness of a nondescript face, wondering how much it had suffered in transmission to a distant fax machine.

"From this?"

"It's what we've got," Casale said. "I'd like it better if we had the bastard's head here on the desk, but we move on and work with what we have."

"Of course."

"So, are you in, or do you want to stay behind and hold the fort?"

Bewildered by Casale's slang, al-Rachid said, "I will go with you. Assuming you have space, that is."

"You kidding me? We got a Super Puma. That's—"

"A helicopter now made by Eurocopter," al-Rachid interrupted. "The 322 Super Puma, with seating for twenty-one passengers."

"Right." Casale looked surprised. "That's pretty good."

"We don't all ride on camels."

"Uh-huh. Whatever. So you're in?" Casale queried.

"I am. Together with my men, of course."

"What say we each take half our guys, and leave the others here to cover San José?"

"That seems wise," al-Rachid agreed.

"Okay, it's set, then. Chopper's on the way. We should be out of here in fifteen, tops."

"Minutes?"

"What else?"

Al-Rachid was moving toward the study's doorway as he said, "I must alert my men."

"Sure thing. Don't want them short on anything."

Al-Rachid ignored Casale's parting comment, left the study door wide-open as he moved along the corridor past hard-eyed body-guards. His men were ready, more or less. Nothing to do but grab their weapons and line up to board the aircraft.

In his head, al-Rachid selected those who would accompany him. Four out of eight, which left him all the more outnumbered by Sicilians. If anything went wrong…

He caught himself at that.

If anything went wrong, al-Rachid assumed that it would be Casale's fault. In a worst-case scenario, it might be each man for himself.

So be it, al-Rachid thought. As Allah wills.

9

Cordillera de Guanacaste,
Costa Rica

The oil light had turned out to be no problem, after all. Nothing that a
top-off at Barranca's main-drag service station couldn't fix. Bolan had
purchased gasoline at the same stop and supervised Gil Favor's visit to
the tiny men's room. Within half an hour, they were on their way, for-
tified by junk food from the station's shiny new vending machine.

"Liberia's the next town?" Bolan asked his navigator.

"Sixty-five miles," Blanca Herrera replied. "An hour, more or less."

"Should be no problem," Bolan said, sounding more confident
than he felt.

It seemed to him that people had been watching them during their
pit stop in Barranca. Maybe that was normal treatment for a gringo
tourist, so far from the capital, but it made Bolan wonder if there might
be spies in place, reporting back to someone who would take their information and digest it, then dispatch a team of soldiers to investigate.

That all takes time, he told himself, but time was relative. It took
only a moment for an order to be passed, and if the troops were
standing by, they could be mobilized in nothing flat. An airborne team
could beat him to the border, even if they hadn't boarded choppers yet.

But Bolan wasn't going to the border.

He was headed for a ghost town, a rendezvous with Jack Grimaldi
and a safe flight home.

Unless his opposition had a mole at Stony Man, there was no way
on Earth they could anticipate that move. If they looked northward,

which was natural enough, and started trolling on the highway, Bolan could elude them when he went to ground.

"What can you tell me about Agua Caliente?" he asked Herrera.

"Well, you understand the name?"

"Hot water. So?"

"There is a sulfur spring, or was. No great surprise, considering there are several volcanoes found in these mountains. Arenal, off to the west in the Cordillera de Tilarán, is one of the world's most active today. Hot springs are not uncommon here."

"But Agua Caliente was a special case," he guessed.

"Indeed," she answered, smiling. "Many years ago, before the First World War, some peasant children had a vision of the Holy Mother, floating in the clouds above the village. Others claimed to see it also. Soon the place was overrun by people who believed the springs could cure their many ailments, even make them young again."

"Like Fatima," Bolan said.

"Or a dozen other places you could name," Herrera replied. "Surprisingly, it seemed to work for many people. I believe the sulfuric springs have certain healing powers of their own, while others come from here." She raised a hand and tapped her temple with the index finger.

"So, no miracles?" Bolan asked.

"There were many claims, of course, but no more sightings of the Virgin. Then, around the same time that your president was killed in Texas, some visitors to Agua Caliente had another vision."

"Oh?"

"It was the Devil this time, so they claimed. Five strangers to one another witnessed Satan rising from water of the hot springs, mouthing curses in a language that they could not understand."

"How did they recognize the curses, then?" Bolan asked.

"Intuition, I suppose." Herrera smiled. "Then again, what else would Satan do?"

"Maybe he dropped in for a treatment," Bolan offered. "Maybe he was on vacation. I imagine sulfur springs are cooler than the atmosphere he's used to."

That made Herrera laugh. "Perhaps," she said. "In any case, the story spread, and naturally, the faithful who had come before now stayed away. Within a year or so, the town itself was dead, its people gone."

"The springs?" he asked her.

"Flow as always, I suppose. I've never been there, but the story is well-known."

"How likely is it that we'll run into an accidental tourist?"

Herrera shrugged at that. "Unlikely," she replied, "but not impossible. I've never heard of any squatters living there. The village has an evil reputation."

"Just the sort of thing that draws teenage adventurers," Bolan observed.

"Perhaps in the United States," she said. "For many here in Costa Rica, faith and superstition have a stronger grip, I think."

"Let's hope so," Bolan answered. "Witnesses are one thing we don't need. And if there's trouble, I don't want civilians getting in the way."

"Does that include yours truly?" Favor asked from the backseat.

"You're in for the duration," Bolan told his captive, "but I'm hoping you have sense enough to stay out of the line of fire."

"Oh, you can count on that," Favor said. "If I have a choice."

"Then keep your fingers crossed. Maybe we won't have any company in Agua Caliente but the ghosts."

"Oh, don't say that!" Herrera protested as she crossed herself.

"I didn't know you were religious," Bolan answered.

"What's your saying in America, about no atheists in foxholes?"

"Right. I hear you."

"Anyway," she said, "a small prayer couldn't hurt."

You got that right, Bolan thought. But he kept it to himself.

New York City

"WE'VE GOT A LEAD," Armand Casale said over the phone, a bare hint of excitement in his voice. "I wanted you to know, first thing."

Tony Romano sipped his bourbon, shifting restlessly against the padded leather of his armchair. "So, what is it?" he demanded.

"Spotters on the highway north of San José checked in,"

Casale said. Some kind of noise in the background nearly drowned out his words.

"So, what's the tip?"

"Two gringos and a woman in a car, way off the beaten track. The eyes are pretty sure one of them was the guy who beat us to the mark."

"Beat *you*," Romano said, correcting him. "What does 'pretty sure' mean?"

"We got a picture off his phony driver's license, from the rental agency. I faxed it up to this Barranca place and got a pretty good ID."

"And Favor?"

"Well, I don't have any pictures of him, but the spotter gave a fair description, age and all."

"You said three people."

"There's a woman riding with them," Casale explained. "Probably some kind of cop."

"You need to clean this up, Armand. I don't mind telling you, it's been a sloppy, disappointing piece of work so far."

"Yes, sir. I'm right on top of it."

"And what's that goddamned noise?"

"We're in a chopper, boss. Headed for Barranca where the runner was last spotted."

"You got the ragheads with you?" Romano asked.

"Five of them," Casale said. "The rest are all our boys."

"Don't let them get involved in any weird religious shit, or whatever they do," Romano warned. "I want this thing cleaned up for good, tonight."

"I hear you, boss."

"But do you understand me?"

"Yes, sir. Clear as crystal."

"Good. Just so we're positively on the same wavelength," Romano said, "if you can't do this thing for any reason—I don't care if it's the weather or a fucking act of God—don't bother coming back."

"I'll get it done," Casale promised, his contrition nearly swallowed by the noise Romano recognized, belatedly, as helicopter rotors.

"Do that," Romano said, and severed the connection without any pointless niceties.

"What did he say?" asked John Fabrizio, reclining on a matching leather sofa.

"Some hot tip," Romano answered, "from a town I never heard of. If they're right, then Favor's headed north."

"What's north?" Fabrizio inquired.

"Mountains and shit, I think," Romano answered. "Pissant towns all up and down there. Nicaragua."

"What the hell would Favor do in Nicaragua?"

"Hide. Pay off the locals like he did in Costa Rica. How the hell should I know? Maybe he's just passing through."

"And then what?"

"Look, I'm not a fucking mind reader, okay?"

"Okay." Fabrizio raised open palms, a gesture of surrender.

"What about al-Bari?" Romano asked. "What's he up to with his people?"

"I have trouble reading that one, Tony. But there's something. Like he's got a big pot on the stove, but dinner isn't ready yet. You know?"

"Jesus. The last thing that we need right now is any more fanatic shit to agitate the Feds. If he's got something in the works, we need to find out what it is and stop it."

"There's an easy way to do that, Tone."

Take out al-Bari, right.

"Let's hold that back for now, until we know exactly what he's up to."

"You're the boss."

"Put somebody on him, and I mean 24/7."

"What about his people?"

"How many are there, again?"

"The top dogs, three or four," Fabrizio said. "Soldiers? We never kept track."

"The lieutenants, then," Romano said. "He won't trust phones to pass an order for the kind of shit we're talking, right?"

"I doubt it, boss."

"Okay, then. Track 'em, keep me posted, and if anything starts going down that could blow back on us, prevent it."

"Take 'em out?"

Romano nodded. "What the hell?" he said. "We may come out of this as heroes, after all."

Washington, D.C.

BROGNOLA COULD HAVE waited for the news, but waiting made him old before his time. That was his theory, anyway. The scrambled sat phone purred in his left ear. After one ring, Grimaldi answered.

"Yeah?"

"It's only me," Brognola said.

"What's up, Chief?"

"I'm just checking in. Where are you?"

"Coming up on Yucatán," Grimaldi said. "I have to land there and refuel. With any luck, they should be ready for me and it won't take long."

"Okay. What word from our friend?"

"I've got coordinates for the connection," Grimaldi said, "but the timing's iffy. They're ahead of me, or were, the last I heard."

"So, where's the hookup?" Brognola asked.

"A place called Agua Caliente, near the border," the ace pilot replied. "It's supposed to be a ghost town, if you can believe it."

"And when you pick them up, it's back to San José?"

"To get the Lear. That's right. I'll have it fueled and waiting for the turnaround," Grimaldi said.

"And then it's, what, about six hours back to JFK?"

"With fueling stops," Grimaldi said. "If Mother Nature's on our side."

"Okay, I'll see you in New York, then."

"It's a date," Grimaldi said, and broke the link.

Brognola dialed the Farm again, got Aaron Kurtzman on the line and started double-checking their arrangements with officials in the Costa Rican capital. The chopper was indeed on standby, fueled and waiting for Grimaldi. They had not been able to obtain a military gunship, in the circumstances, but Brognola trusted the Stony Man pilot to make the best of what they had.

That done, he swept the papers off his desk and locked them in a desk drawer, where they wouldn't tempt the Justice building's cleaning crew, and called it a night.

New York City

KASIM AL-BARI SIPPED a steaming cup of herbal tea and considered his options. His faith denied him any alcoholic beverage, but al-Bari hardly needed artificial stimulants to agitate him in the present circumstances.

He was on a deadline, with the emphasis on *dead*.

It had been too long since the Sword of Allah struck a telling blow against America or its allies. He didn't count the Costa Rican bombing, since he had not ordered it and no conceivable distortion of the truth could link it to his war against Israel or Washington. It was a chapter to be closed and then forgotten.

On the other hand, he had a project in development on U.S. soil, nearing fruition even as al-Bari sat and drank his tea. The strike had been postponed after Romano was indicted, when the headlines broke about a Mafia connection to "extreme Islamic fundamentalists." Eliminating witnesses had seemed to be the top priority, but now al Bari had begun to think that he should leave Romano to sink or swim on his own.

Romano's fate no longer interested al-Bari. From all appearances, the gangster had outlived his usefulness. Publicity and federal indictments would prevent Romano from supplying any more matériel or vital information to the Sword. He had become an albatross around al-Bari's neck, concerned primarily—and understandably, of course— with personal concerns, including prospects of a lifetime in a cage.

Too bad.

Al-Bari hated all Americans, except those Muslim converts who betrayed their homeland for the greater good of Allah—and, in truth, he had great difficulty trusting even them. He lived to wound the Great Satan that nourished and supported Israel, waging ruthless war against Islamic countries.

Wound it, or kill it, if he could.

That task might be beyond his capabilities, but he would strive relentlessly for any goal within his reach, then curse the hated enemy with his last breath.

The strike al-Bari had in mind would hurt America beyond all doubt. It would reopen wounds inflicted by the martyrs who had come before al-Bari, those who lived eternally in sacred memories.

Al-Bari was not named in the indictments that had placed Antonio Romano's life in jeopardy. The oversight perplexed him, but it hardly mattered to al-Bari whether he was listed on some legal document. The FBI would have arrested him by now if it could find him. Someday, it might happen, but he still had time to strike another blow.

Al-Bari hadn't raised the subject with Romano, knowing the Sicilian would object. Worried about his trial and bad publicity, Romano might even attempt to stop him, which would be unfortunate for all concerned.

But much could happen while the mobster was distracted. By the time Romano heard of it, the strike would be another bit of history—and so, perhaps, would the Romano Family.

"Progress reports," al-Bari said, sweeping his gaze across the solemn faces of his three most trusted aides in the United States. Haroun al-Rachid would have joined them, as first among equals, if not for the distraction of his work in Costa Rica.

First to answer, on al Bari's left, was slender Mukhtar Fahd. "All is in readiness with the munitions and explosives," he replied. "I have six men prepared to strike on your command."

"And how much notice is required?" al-Bari asked.

"No more than sixty minutes."

"Excellent." Al-Bari turned his gaze to Karif Gadi. "Next. The target?"

"As you know," Gadi began, "debate over the form of a Ground Zero monument has occupied our enemies for seven years. They argue endlessly among themselves. Some in their media even attack the widows of the great September raid as allies of our movement. They are very strange."

"The target, please."

"Yes, sir. At last, construction has begun, though barely. Striking now, before they make progress, affirms that they cannot erase the scars inflicted by Allah."

"We are agreed." Another shift. "And lastly?"

Butrus Al-Dabir looked duly solemn as he said, "There will be no escape for martyrs, but I have prepared safehouses for the four of us in Canada. Our new identities are already in place. We may step into them at any time."

"No reason for delay, then? None at all?" al-Bari asked.

His three lieutenants shook their heads.

"We shall proceed on schedule, then," he told them. "But be careful of our so-called friends. If the Sicilians try to interfere in any way, destroy them."

Cordillera de Tilarán

ARMAND CASALE HATED helicopters, but the men around him wouldn't know it from his casual demeanor or the way he peered through his window at the treetops skimming past below them. Flying didn't bother him, per se, but sitting in an airship that could drop vertically like a stone from the sky tied his guts into knots.

Too freaking bad.

Orders were orders, and Romano hadn't stuttered when he spelled them out. Succeed, or don't come back. There'd been no need to add the punch line, that Casale's name would be the next one listed on a murder contract if he failed to bag Gil Favor and the pricks who'd helped him get away.

Except, one of them *wasn't* a prick, after all.

One of them was a bitch.

Casale didn't know exactly how she factored in, but all the federal agencies hired women now. He supposed that most of them were competent, within their limits, but he'd never met a woman who could match a man where killing was concerned.

"Five minutes to Barranca," the pilot announced, his voice sounding robotic in the earphones that Casale wore.

He braced himself for the descent, looking ahead to their interrogation of the local witness and whatever followed. It was probably too much to hope that they'd find Favor and the others still in town. A stop for oil meant they were moving out and onward—but toward what?

Could Favor's escorts really plan on driving all the way from Costa Rica to the States? Casale didn't think it probable.

Al-Rachid's bombers had missed them at the San José airport, but they'd taken out the right plane, anyway. Scared off from trying a commercial flight, Favor and his companions would've tried some alternate arrangement. That, in turn, had put them on the road.

But going where?

Casale felt his stomach lurch as they began descending toward an open field located on the southern outskirts of Barranca.

It was almost funny, when he thought about it. Thirty minutes earlier, he'd never heard the name of this town, didn't know that it existed. Now the key to his survival might be found here, resting in the hands of a Latino grease monkey.

Hilarious.

Casale's roiling stomach settled as the chopper touched down. He doffed the earphones and unstrapped the so-called safety harness, which he'd known would be no help at all if they plummeted to Earth.

Ready.

Casale wore a hidden pistol, like the other members of his team. Their real artillery was packed in gym bags, stowed as luggage, out of sight, in case some nosy cop came sniffing around. Casale didn't know if Costa Rican law required probable cause for a search, but he had bullets waiting for any dumb flatfoot who got in his way.

Lazaro's man was waiting for them with a car. One car, for twenty guys. He seemed surprised as they unloaded from the helicopter, one by one.

"Where's the garage?" he asked.

"Not far," the spotter answered. "Just downtown. I am afraid… this car…is not enough."

"Forget about it," Casale said. Turning to the team, he beckoned Haroun al-Rachid and two of his own men to join him in the car, then focused on the driver once again and said, "Let's go."

It was a short journey, as advertised. Casale counted off six blocks before they pulled into a service station's parking lot. The place was blacked out for the night, except for one light burning in the office, where a worried-looking local sat behind a cheap desk, shooting glances at a short, mean-looking man in a suit who occupied a corner, near the exit.

Yet another of Lazaro's men, Casale reasoned. They were on the job, at least, ensuring that the witness didn't skip. Whether his story would be worth the trip from San José was something else again.

There's only one way to find out, Casale thought, and trailed their driver through the office door.

"All right," he said, when they were all inside the crowded room. "Let's hear it."

10

Mérida, Yucatán, Mexico

The service crew was slower than Grimaldi would've liked, but there was very little he could do about it. Glaring gringos didn't have a lot of weight to throw around in Yucatán, unless they traveled with a caravan of native troops or *federales*.

The Stony Man pilot was short of both, and didn't want to start the time-consuming wrangling that would be inevitable if he offered bribes for faster service, so he waited. He used the downtime to review his charts and double-check coordinates for Agua Caliente through his GPS.

It didn't show on any of his maps, which came as no surprise if the inhabitants had bailed out long ago. Grimaldi's charts and maps were always up-to-date, the latest he could find. Ghost towns abandoned generations in the past would only register if they were active tourist draws. Without the constant traffic, as Grimaldi knew from personal experience, the jungle could reclaim a former human settlement with startling rapidity.

So would he actually find a place to land at Agua Caliente, or would he be forced to fake it, hovering above the LZ, dropping lines and harnesses?

He'd specified the whirlybird in San José with a winch that would allow him to lower cargo from a hover or go fishing for passengers on terrain where landing was ill-advised. Of course, he'd have to operate the gear from his seat in the cockpit while flying solo, but Grimaldi wouldn't trust a foreign copilot he'd picked up on the fly.

Grimaldi put his maps away and tried to visualize his destination. It came out looking like a hundred other jungle LZs where he'd made deliveries or pickups in the past, and that was fine. Each had its problems and its dangers.

The Stony Man ace wondered if the access roads to Agua Caliente had been maintained and would be passable for vehicles. If not, it meant that Bolan and his two companions would be forced to hike in, losing time. Grimaldi knew his old friend would've thought about that first, considered it when he was estimating their arrival time.

Which meant that it was not Grimaldi's problem.

He had other things to think about. The helicopter, first, and then the weapons Stony Man had promised to have waiting for him when he reached his takeoff point in San José. Although it used up precious time, he'd need to taxi from the city's airport to a private strip that rented choppers by the hour or the day. There'd been no question of delivering the hardware he required to San José International, much less installing it aboard a sedate civilian aircraft, but money talked.

What the local law didn't know wouldn't hurt Grimaldi.

Ten minutes later the Stony Man pilot was airborne in the Learjet, streaking southeastward for Quintana Roo and the Gulf of Honduras beyond. Grimaldi wished he could accelerate beyond the Learjet's built-in limits, but technology could only do so much.

He should be on the ground in San José sometime within the next two hours. Then came the cab ride and inspection of the chopper waiting for him at the private strip, arranged by Stony Man.

"Better be right," Grimaldi muttered to himself, fists clenching restlessly on the controls.

Liberia, Costa Rica

"WHAT'S FUNNY?" Herrera asked.

"Nothing," Bolan answered.

"You were smiling," she informed him, "as if someone told a joke."

"The joke's on us," Bolan answered. "We're in Costa Rica, driving through a town named for a state in Africa. The Mafia is chasing us, maybe with Arab terrorists, and we're all heading for a ghost town. That's about the size of it."

"I find none of this reassuring," she said.

"No," he agreed. "I wouldn't call it that."

"I understand it's difficult with the police," she said, "because of *him*—"

"I have a name," Favor said, interrupting from the backseat. "And I'm not exactly deaf."

Herrera ignored his protest and pressed on. "But there still must be someone we can trust to help us."

Bolan nodded. "He's already on the way. With any luck, after the time we lost back in Barranca, we won't have too long to wait."

"One man," she said.

"One hell of a soldier and sky jockey," Bolan corrected the lady. "If he can't lift us out, nobody can."

"And if," she said, "that proves to be the case?"

The warrior shook his head. "Don't say that. Hell, don't even *think* it. Any step you take can be your last, but if you let that get inside your head and set up housekeeping, you're done before you start."

"I should be optimistic, then?" she asked with just a note of sarcasm.

"It couldn't hurt," Bolan replied. "What do you have to lose?"

"You think they are already tracking us," she said. It didn't come out sounding like a question.

"If they're not," Bolan said, "then they've dropped the ball bigtime. They ought to cover the escape routes, even if they think we're still in San José."

"And it will hurt us, stopping in Barranca."

"Maybe. But it would've hurt us more to let the car die while we're still short of the pickup."

"Agua Caliente," Herrera almost whispered.

"Right. The ghost town."

"Listen," Favor chimed in from the rear. "I really do appreciate you being all gung-ho and everything, but can you stop and *think* for just a second here?"

"Save it," Bolan responded, meeting Favor's flat gaze in the rearview mirror.

"No, I'm serious," the fugitive replied. "I'm guessing that the two of you don't really want to die. I know *I* don't. Why not just let me go, and get rich on the side? Tell whoever it is you're working for that I outwitted you. What can they do but fire you, anyway? A couple million dollars in your pocket. You don't need the crappy job."

"Can't do it," Bolan said.

"You mean *won't* do it," Favor answered.

"Take your pick. I'm thinking, like you asked me to. It just won't fly."

"Why not? I mean, your great morality aside?"

"I'm being practical," Bolan explained, "not self-righteous. Even if we let you go, Romano's people won't stop hunting you."

"My problem," Favor said. "I'm filthy rich, you may recall. Suppose they nail me in another six months, or a year. At least I'll have that time. Locked up, I won't last through the week."

"You'll have protection," Bolan said.

"Uh-huh. Because it's just *so* safe in custody."

"There's something else," Bolan replied. "Romano's people wouldn't know that we released you. They'd keep hunting us, as well."

"Put up a goddamned billboard," their captive said. "Favor Got Away. Buy ads on television. Call the bastard, if you want to. I still know his private number, if he hasn't changed it."

"Nope," Bolan said. "If we've got the risks, regardless, then we might as well stay on the job."

Favor leaned forward, fastening his eyes on Blanca Herrera. "Does he speak for you, too? You're not even from the States. What do you care whether Romano goes away or not? It can't mean anything to you."

"I like to sleep at night," she said.

"And hiding out from Tony's crew is so conducive to your beauty sleep? Okay, I get it. Both of you play by the book. But, hey—that's not true, either, is it? Maybe you're afraid of getting picked up for the killings and the other shit you've done."

"That's not your problem," Bolan said.

"Now pull the other one, so I can walk without a limp," Favor retorted, then he slumped back in his seat. "Jesus, the two of you are just alike. Hopeless."

Not yet, Bolan thought, but he said, "There's always hope."

Favor made no reply, and that was fine. Bolan had more important things to think about than their prisoner's state of mind.

Like getting to the ghost town, finding someplace they could safely hide and waiting for Grimaldi to arrive.

Barranca

IT MADE ARMAND CASALE nervous, feeding questions to the grease monkey and waiting for them to be translated, then waiting out the slow and rambling responses. Hell, he didn't even know if the interpreter Lazaro had supplied was playing straight with them or not. Granted, the guy had no apparent motive for deceiving them— nothing to gain, and everything to lose—but Casale was suspicious by nature, and the day's events had only made him more so.

Bit by bit, they pried the information out of the mechanic. Descriptions of the gringo men and a sketchy image of the woman who traveled with them. The mechanic thought she was a Costa Rican native, probably because she did the talking in his language.

Which proved nothing, by the way, but there was no point arguing about such trivia. Casale didn't care if she was Costa Rican, Mexican or Red Chinese, as long as he could frame her in his gun sights. Take her down, along with Favor and the other prick who'd made his life so miserable lately.

Once they had confirmed their targets, Casale focused on the car. According to his witness, it was an expensive SUV, painted in a color that the stateside manufacturer would likely call champagne, or some weird shit. It had been low on oil when they pulled in, but had no leaks or other damage that should slow it.

Needless to say, the slack-jawed yokel hadn't bothered glancing at the license tags, much less committing them to memory. Why should he, when he had no reason to believe that anybody cared about two gringos and a Costa Rican passing through?

Casale knew that they had left town, heading north, without a mention of their final destination. It was better than a swift kick in the nuts, but still frustrating. Did they have some kind of rendezvous arranged, the goddamned cavalry awaiting them?

Or were they simply running for their lives?

Casale finally decided that it made no difference. He had to find them quickly, and to hell with what they had in mind. He handed money to Lazaro's soldier, for the witness, and stalked out into the darkness with Haroun al-Rachid on his heels.

"What now?" the Arab asked.

Casale answered with a question of his own. "What else? If we keep chasing them, not knowing where they're headed, then we have to stop and check every turnoff from here to the border. Hell, from here to the States. It only works if we can head them off."

"The helicopter," al-Rachid said, seeing the way it had to go.

Casale nodded. "Right. We send the bird ahead to scout the highway. If it spots them, it can slow them down. Meanwhile, we're rolling up behind."

"On foot?" al-Rachid inquired. "The car we have—"

"Won't do the job," Casale cut him off. "I know."

Lazaro's man emerged from the gas station, brushing past the others. He approached Casale with a bland expression on his face, shooting little sidelong glances toward al-Rachid. The guy was trying to figure out who really ran the show. Casale didn't want to leave him any doubt.

"I need more cars," he said. "Enough for fifteen men. I need them right away."

Lazaro's man blinked once at him, then nodded. "Certainly, *señor*. Vehicles can be found, but in Barranca, at this time of night—"

Casale interrupted him. "I don't have time for lame excuses here. Your boss put us in touch for a specific purpose, to complete a certain job. It's not done yet, and won't be done until I find the three people your boy described in there. Find them and stop them cold."

"I understand, of course."

"Then you can get the wheels."

"It shall be done."

"How long?"

The local took another moment to consider, then replied, "No more than half an hour, *señor*."

Casale saw no point in pushing it. "Okay," he said. "Let's get it done."

Lazaro's man went scuttling off as al-Rachid asked him, "You will go on with the helicopter, then?"

Casale checked the Arab's face for any hint of sneering sarcasm before he answered. "No. I'm staying here to make sure that the cars come through on time and everybody's organized, no jerking off."

"Then you won't mind if I—"

"Sorry," Casale cut him off. He had already seen the trap that lay in front of him, al-Rachid showboating it and claiming credit for the kill to balance out his epic fuckup at the airport. "I'll need you," Casale said, "to give your boys their orders when the time comes."

"All my *men* speak English," al-Rachid countered.

"No kidding? All I ever hear them speaking is their home lingo. Anyway, I'd still feel better if you stuck around. I'm sending Rocco up ahead with four, five men to check things out."

Al-Rachid seemed on the verge of arguing, but didn't follow through. "Of course," he said. "As you prefer."

"That's settled, then," Casale said. "Let's get this show back on the road."

Cordillera de Guanacaste

"ACCORDING TO THE MAP," Herrera remarked, "it should be roughly half an hour now before we see the road to Agua Caliente."

"If we see it," Favor answered from the backseat. "It's dark out, if you hadn't noticed, and you're looking for a road that used to serve a ghost town sixty years ago. What's wrong with this picture?"

"The sound track," Cooper replied. "If you can't help, you need to be quiet."

"No problem," Favor told him. "You want quiet? I can give you quiet. I can give you quiet all night long."

Herrera saw Cooper glare at Favor in the rearview mirror, but he made no further comment, and their prisoner at last fell into sullen silence.

"We'll just have to keep our eyes peeled," Cooper told her. "My friend has the coordinates, so finding it's no problem. But we may still have to defend ourselves before he gets there, if Romano's people find it first."

"I'm hoping that won't happen," she answered.

"That makes two of us, but be prepared."

"I will."

She thought again of how Matt Cooper's life had to be, if this was all he did. Pursuing fugitives. Fleeing from gunmen bent on killing him. Was that a life?

And yet, as far as she could tell, the man harbored no serious regrets. He didn't seem depressed, or even very apprehensive about their present circumstances. Even in the frenzied heat of battle, she had noticed, the American seemed almost calm.

"How do you do it?" Herrera asked at last.

"Do what?" Cooper inquired.

"Remain so…easygoing, when your life may be in danger?"

"Years of practice," he replied. "There's no advantage to be found in agitation. It'll raise your blood pressure and spoil your aim, but otherwise…"

"You make it sound so easy. Effortless."

"I wouldn't go that far."

"Is there no fear inside you, then?"

"There's plenty," Cooper said. "Fear keeps you sharp and on your toes, but it can also be controlled. That's where experience comes in."

"I understand," she said. "I'm—how is it you say, this—green?"

"That's what we say," Cooper acknowledged. "But you've done all right so far."

"Thank you."

"If you two want to get a room," Favor said, "I can sleep out in the car. Just leave the keys, old boy, so I can play the radio."

"What happened to that vow of silence?" Cooper asked him.

"Just ignore me. Make believe that I'm not even here."

Herrera spoke up before Bolan could respond. "In Agua Caliente, how can we defend a town?" she asked.

"Depends on what we find when we get there," Cooper answered.

"After all these years, there likely won't be much town left. We need an LZ first, and then—"

"LZ?"

"A landing zone. The chopper needs to set down somewhere, or he'll have to reel us in like fish, one at a time."

"I see."

"Beyond that," Cooper told her, "I'll be happy with a place that has four solid walls, a roof over our heads. We can defend most any building, if the odds against us aren't too heavy and the firefight doesn't run too long."

"Your friend can land if there is fighting?" Herrera asked.

"He'll find a way," Cooper replied. "With any luck, he might even pitch in and help."

"If you mean fighting from the helicopter, there are serious restrictions on such weapons and equipment in my country," Herrera said. It sounded foolish to her, even as she said it, with the bags of outlawed hardware sitting at her feet.

"Where there's a will…"

"There is a way," she said, forcing a smile. "I know that saying, too."

Behind them, Favor muttered, "What's that noise?"

Herrera half turned to face him, saying, "What noise?"

"Wait," Cooper said, hushing her. "I hear it, too."

"CHRIST, IT'S DARK DOWN there! You people need some highway lights or something."

Peering through the helicopter's windscreen, trying to survey the mountain road below, Rocco Lampone couldn't see a goddamned thing. For all he knew, there could be dinosaurs dancing the tango down there, and he'd never know it.

"No moon out tonight," the pilot said by way of explanation.

"What was your first clue?" Lampone asked sarcastically.

Dim lights inside the chopper didn't help. The instruments in front of him gave off enough light to guarantee that most of what Lampone saw, when he peered through the window, was his own bug-eyed reflection.

It was an honor, being chosen by Armand Casale as his point man for the hunt, and Lampone didn't want to blow it just because of something stupid, like the laws of science that prevented him from spotting enemies in total darkness.

He knew they were looking for a champagne-colored SUV with three live targets in it. How hard could it be to spot one of those gas-guzzlers out here, on a night like this, when Batman couldn't drive without his headlights?

What he didn't know, of course, was whether they were headed in the right direction to begin with, or if they'd already passed their target, lurking in the darkness below. For all Lampone knew, the target could've headed east or west instead of north. And even if they had the right direction, all the driver had to do was find a turnout, kill his lights and let them pass him by.

Too easy, Lampone thought, but how in hell could he check side roads that he couldn't even see? If they had come equipped with some of that night-vision gear he'd seen in movies, then they'd have a chance. But as it was, forget about it.

But he couldn't. He was under orders, and he had to do the job or take a hit for failing. Maybe even take a dirt nap, if Casale went off on him, though it was supposed to be against the rules for him to whack a made guy without going through the normal, mandatory steps with Don Romano.

Trouble was, nothing about this job was normal. Ever since their flight touched down in Costa Rica, Lampone noted things had gone from bad to worse. A relatively simple hit had gone south with a vengeance, costing lives, and now Lampone had a feeling that all bets were off. If he screwed up, Casale might just take him out and think about the downside later, when he got back home.

Lampone had four soldiers with him, all of them alert and staring out their windows, all of them presumably as blind as he was. If they spotted anything, their orders were to check it out, confirm ID and stop the car if possible.

No sweat.

Except they had to find it first.

"How long until we hit the border?" Lampone asked their pilot.

Glancing at his instruments, the pilot replied, "Another fifteen minutes."

Lampone wasn't cleared to cross the frontier into Nicaragua. In fact, Casale had expressly forbidden risking an international incident. That meant they had a quarter of an hour, give or take, to find their target, then he'd have to turn around and run a search the other way, see if they'd missing something.

Or just admit that he had failed.

No, thanks.

Lampone wasn't sure about the chopper's speed, but knew it had to be better than a hundred miles per hour. Even though he'd sucked at math in school, working the loan-shark trade and numbers banks for Don Romano let him figure out that they were covering just over one and a half miles per minute.

The fifteen-minute deadline put them roughly twenty-five miles from the border. He had that time, that distance, in which to get lucky.

Or else.

And just like that, his wish came true.

"What's that?" Lampone asked the pilot, pointing urgently. "You see that light up there?"

"Headlamps," the pilot said, indifferent.

"That's what I thought," Lampone said. He felt like cheering, but it would've been unseemly. "Let's go down and check 'em out."

The pilot gave a microscopic nod and answered, *"Sí, señor."*

Rocco Lampone turned and flashed a circled thumb and forefinger at his four soldiers.

"Lock and load," he told them, shouting to be heard about the helicopter's noise. "I think we've got a live one."

11

As soon as Bolan recognized the helicopter's whupping sound, he killed the headlights on his stolen SUV. That brought a little gasp from Herrera and a curse from Favor, as the pitch-black night enveloped them.

"Hang on and keep your fingers crossed," he told them, hands rock-steady on the steering wheel.

He didn't tap the brake pedal, which would've made his taillights flare and canceled any benefit he may have gained by going dark. In fact, he thought that it was probably too late for simple tricks, believed the chopper should've spotted them at least a mile off in the night, but he was bound to try.

His faint hope was dashed as a spotlight beam swept across the mountain road in front of them, tracking from left to right and back again, then pinned them squarely in its glare.

So much for luck.

The shooting didn't start immediately. Bolan guessed there'd be some question with the hunters, as to whether they had spotted the right car, but as he understood Tony Romano and his kind, that hesitation wouldn't last for long. Better to kill some innocents, a mafioso would reason, than risk allowing enemies to slip away.

"We need to blind them," he told Herrera. "Can you handle it?"

"Blind them?" Frightened, she clearly didn't understand.

"Before they blow us off the road, we need to kill that spotlight. Can you do it?"

"Maybe," she replied. "I'm not sure, but I'll try."

"Oh my God!" Favor moaned.

"Don't try with the pistol," Bolan counseled. "Use one of the long guns. Once you start it, they'll be shooting back."

"All right." Her voice was determined as she rummaged through the duffels at her feet.

Bolan suppressed a smile as Herrera made the best choice possible, the Steyr AUG assault rifle that he had purchased with the Uzi and their other lethal gear soon after his arrival in San José. The Steyr had the greatest range of any gun on board, was capable of 3-round bursts and had an optic sight that should assist her in her task.

Unless the airborne shooters tagged her first or blinded her with their spotlight.

Bolan tapped a button on the SUV's console and heard a rush of wind as the sunroof's deeply tinted panel whispered open. Whether anyone would notice in the chopper, Bolan couldn't guess, but the roof hatch was Herrera's only realistic hope for taking out the chopper's spotlight—and maybe the aircraft itself.

She checked the Steyr over quickly, demonstrating that she knew the weapon fairly well, then swiveled in her seat and rose to her knees, stretching until her head, shoulders and weapon cleared the sunroof.

Bolan saw the first reaction to her gambit in the wobbling spotlight, but she fired before the whirlybird could veer away. A 3-round burst, as Bolan would've done himself, but then the helicopter veered erratically off course, away to Bolan's left.

However briefly, they were rolling through the dark again. Bolan accelerated, knowing they would only have a short respite, hoping to make the most of it.

"Damn it!" The sound of Herrera's bitter curse was almost swept away. She ducked and told him, needlessly, "I missed. They're gone."

"Not far," he cautioned. "Track them. Now they're sure it's us, they'll come back fighting."

"Jesus Christ!" Favor groaned in the rear. "You bring me all the way out here to get me killed?"

"You're not dead yet," Bolan said.

"I could've been in Argentina now," Favor complained. "The Nazis really aren't so bad. All right, the food's a little heavy, but unless you absolutely have a need to argue politics—"

The spotlight's reappearance silenced him, half blinding Bolan as it swept in from his left, forcing him to close that eye against the sudden glare. Overhead, he heard Herrera firing again, measured bursts with no feeling of panic about them, despite what he knew had to be raging emotions on her part.

"Hold steady," he whispered. "Hold steady and squeeze."

The chopper passed over them, its spotlight more or less steady, while gunfire hammered in answer to Herrera's. She squealed but kept firing, hips and legs swiveling in Bolan's peripheral vision as she tried to keep up with the swooping aircraft.

She was doing all right, Bolan thought. Still no hit on the spotlight, but their enemies had missed the SUV completely on their strafing run. He had to give Herrera some credit for that, standing tall with her rifle and popping away in the face of their incoming fire.

He wondered which direction they would come from next. Herrera could track them from the sunroof, whatever it was, but her anatomy and the construction of her seat made some angles more awkward than others, slowed her turns as she had to shift knees and feet.

The chopper was beyond his line of sight, but Bolan knew they were coming back when the spotlight tried to blind him. This time it was glaring fully in his face. The whirlybird was coming at them from the north.

Head-on.

"Is that a broad down there?" Rocco Lampone asked of no one in particular.

"Looks like it," someone answered.

"Or a guy with crazy fuckin' hair," someone else said.

"Well, either way, somebody take 'em out!" Lampone commanded, clinging to his seat with both hands as the helicopter pitched and yawed, dodging the bullets rising from the SUV like angry hornets.

Lampone could've sworn that he'd already heard a couple of them strike the chopper's underside, but he was praying that he had that wrong. He didn't even want to think about the fuel lines, the electric cables and the other mechanical hardware that could be damaged by a single bullet, sending all of them into a screaming nosedive to the unforgiving earth below.

They made another low pass at the SUV, his soldiers cutting loose with everything they had. Specifically, that was two shotguns, one MP-5K machine pistol and a stubby carbine version of the classic M-16.

It should've been enough, but they were firing at an awkward angle, from their windows, while the helicopter swooped and swerved. It nearly made Lampone queasy, and he wasn't even firing at the target.

Rounding on the pilot, Lampone bellowed, "Can you hold steady for a minute? Is that too damned much to ask? We're workin' here!"

The pilot blinked at him, clearly surprised, then said, "I try another pass."

"Another steady pass," Lampone instructed him.

"Sí, sí."

The pilot swung them through a wide loop to the east and back around to rush the SUV head-on. Lampone knew it didn't take a rocket scientist or highway engineer to realize that his boys would have a harder time than ever, firing to the front, but that was lost on their chauffeur.

At least he kept the chopper's spotlight centered on the truck's windshield. Maybe its driver would be blinded by the glare. Maybe the wild-haired shooter, too.

But there she was. A broad, for damned sure, with that creamy cleavage showing, but it was the automatic rifle in her hands that claimed his attention. Even with the spotlight blanching out her features, he could see the muzzle-flashes from her weapon when she started firing, holding nice and steady from the look of it.

Spang!

He definitely heard the bullet strike that time, and for a second Lampone worried that he might've soiled himself. He clenched his cheeks, stopped short of feeling for a wet spot on his slacks, toes tightly curled inside his wingtip shoes.

They could be losing fuel or something, right that minute. Nobody would know until the gauges started going crazy, then the bird nosed over and went hurtling toward the ground, crumpling into a twisted mass of flaming wreckage.

He shouted at the pilot. "Did you ever fly this thing before? She's shooting *holes* in it!"

The pilot's voice was almost mocking as he retorted, "You want it steady, or you want it safe?"

"Listen, smart-ass. I wanna do my job and live to tell about it. Which part don't you fucking understand?"

"Evasive flying, not so good for shooting," the pilot said, obviously unimpressed with Lampone's show of anger. "Steady, close-up flying good for shoot both ways. The safest place, straight up above."

"Do that!" Lampone snapped. "Put us directly over them, about a hundred feet, and hold it steady like your life depended on it. Hear me, Pedro?"

"Sí, señor."

The chopper swooped, then soared. A moment later, they were coming up behind the SUV, a hundred-something feet above it, closing in and keeping pace. The spotlight held steady, pinning their target while Lampone fumbled in the bag between his feet and started palming hand grenades.

He had forgotten them, in his excitement, thinking that a pass or two would be enough to run the SUV off the road. Well, he'd been wrong, and if they couldn't strafe the bastards, he could damn well bomb them, couldn't he?

Good question.

As the pilot followed orders, staking out a spot directly over the intended target, Lampone realized he couldn't see the SUV at all. It was below them, as he'd ordered, and there was no window in the chopper's floorboard.

"What do you think?" he asked the pilot, brandishing grenades in both fat hands. "I drop these from the window, will they hit?"

The pilot shrugged. "Hit something," he replied.

Before he pulled the first pin, Lampone saw the loophole in his logic. If the chopper and the SUV were traveling at roughly the same speed, any grenades he dropped would fall behind the speeding car.

Lampone knew he had six seconds from release to detonation, and the SUV could travel how far in that length of time?

"We need to get a little ways ahead of them," he told the pilot. "Otherwise—"

"I understand, *señor*."

Smart bastard wouldn't even let him finish it, just goosed the whirlybird's accelerator, or whatever it was called. They powered forward, rotors whipping at the air above, and Lampone fumbled with his window latch, fingers made awkward by his grip on the grenade.

A heartbeat later, and he got it, sliding the foot-square window back and grimacing at the blast of wind and noise that hit him squarely in the face. It had been loud enough before, with windows open wide behind him, but the new rush made it worse.

He pulled the pin on the grenade in his right hand and stuck his arm through the window, cursing as wind tried to rip it from its socket. Christ! Lampone realized he hadn't thought this through completely, but he had to try, regardless.

"Bombs away," he muttered, and released the frag grenade.

BLANCA HERRERA WAS straining for a shot, back arched, eyes nearly shut against the spotlight's blinding glare. Wind whipped her hair around her face in tangles, stinging when it lashed across her slitted eyes. The helicopter was a looming shape, the silhouette of some huge, prehistoric insect in the blinding light.

It helped a little when the aircraft pulled ahead. Herrera had no idea what they were doing, vaguely conscious that the gunmen in the chopper couldn't fire at her while they were hovering above the SUV, but *she* could fire, and did.

Her finger stroked the rifle's trigger, rattling off one 3-round burst, and then another. She wasn't sure how many rounds the Steyr had left, and she could hardly stop to check its see-through plastic magazine.

Not when she had a chance to bring the helicopter down.

The first explosion shocked her, nearly made her drop the rifle overboard. She screamed involuntarily and ducked as shrapnel struck the SUV along its flank. Inside the cab, she heard a muffled curse from Favor, and Cooper started swerving, left and right.

Herrera ducked lower, rifle still raised through the sunroof, as she called to the big American, "What was that?"

"Grenade, I think," he answered. "Maybe you should—"

"No! I can do this!"

Rising again before he could protest, Herrera was hasty with her next burst, fearing she had wasted it—until the helicopter's spotlight popped, flared brighter for a heartbeat, then went out in a shower of sparks.

She felt like cheering, but restrained herself. The battle wasn't over yet, though Herrera felt that she had placed them on more even ground.

As if in answer to that selfish thought, another hand grenade exploded on the pavement, twenty feet or so in front of their vehicle. Herrera ducked instinctively, recoiling from the blast, and felt some tiny, sharp-edged missile sting her cheek. Blood welled immediately from the gash and warmed her jawline.

Cooper was swerving again, steering a serpentine path along the two-lane mountain road as he tried to dodge the grenade blasts. How many more bombs did their enemies have in the helicopter? she wondered.

Herrera knew she couldn't stop to think about that now. Cursing fluently in Spanish at the adversaries who had scarred her, she shouldered the Steyr again, found her target as it banked to make another pass and squeezed the rifle's trigger. Again and again she squeezed it, rattling off 3-round bursts until the weapon's slide locked open on an empty chamber.

Frantic, she dropped back through the sunroof of the SUV, ditching the rifle's empty magazine and groping for another in the larger of the duffel bags beside her seat. She found one, snapped it into the Steyr's receiver and slammed the bolt home to chamber a round. Before she rose to fire again, she glimpsed Gil Favor staring at her from the backseat floorboard, gaping as if she had gone insane.

To hell with him, she thought. To hell with all of them.

Herrera rose with the rifle already at her shoulder, fired a burst into the chopper's underbelly as it passed above her head, seeming almost close enough to touch with outstretched fingertips.

The next grenade exploded then, a thunderclap of roiling smoke and flame that battered Herrera's eardrums. For an instant, she believed that she was falling, that she'd tipped over the SUV's broad roof somehow, but then she realized that it was Cooper veering toward the western shoulder of the highway, screeching to a halt.

"I GOT 'EM THAT TIME!" Lampone shouted, whooping as he saw the shrapnel-scarred vehicle swerve and shudder to a stop with brake lights flaring. He ordered the pilot, "Make another pass, so we can give 'em hell, then set this turkey down."

Turning toward his soldiers as the chopper banked, he ordered, "Blast the shit out of 'em on this pass, before we land."

Four heads nodded in unison, a couple of them flashing him smiles. They held their weapons ready, anxious to comply.

Winning was good.

Losing, well, losing sucked.

Lampone saw that the SUV would be on his side when they passed it, so he cocked his stubby Ingram MAC-10 stuttergun and thrust it out the window, aiming it as best he could and blazing off the whole damned 32-round magazine at 1,200 rounds per minute.

It was there and gone. Lampone couldn't tell if he had put a single bullet in the target, but he felt elated all the same. This was his victory, and he would get full credit for it from Casale.

And from Don Romano, too.

The chopper banked again, slowing as it approached the stalled-out SUV from the rear, settling lower until they were gliding along only ten feet or so above blacktop. Without the helicopter's spotlight or the truck's headlights, all Lampone saw was a pale sort of lump on the roadside. Dark windows concealed the bitch who'd tried to kill him and her friends.

But not for long.

"All right," he told the pilot. "Set her down."

The words had barely passed his lips when someone rose beside the SUV, along the driver's side. Lampone recoiled, as if the figure had been touching-close, instead of thirty feet away. He cursed as safety belts and the copilot's seat prevented him from ducking out of sight.

"Jesus!"

The muzzle-flashes at that range were unmistakable. Lampone

saw them first, then heard the automatic weapon hammering away at him. Bullets raked the chopper's nose, punched through the windshield, raising sparks from the instrument panel.

Lampone flinched from flying glass and saw the pilot twitching in his shoulder harness, futile hands raised to block the stream of bullets ripping into him. One of the slugs drilled Lampone's shoulder then, the pain incredible, like being skewered with a red-hot poker in a vengeful giant's hands.

The second hit was almost welcome by comparison. It had to have clipped some kind of nerve, since Lampone's arm and shoulder suddenly went numb, like flipping off a pain switch in his head. The shock of impact stunned him, and he guessed the numbness was a bad thing, really, but his mind was focused on the task of getting up and out of there.

Simple. A six-year-old could do it, once you showed him how, but Lampone's fingers weren't obeying orders as they should. His left arm was a write-off, maybe dangling by a thread for all he knew, and when he tried to reach the harness buckle with his right, Lampone slapped himself across the belly with his submachine gun.

"Shit!"

He dropped the weapon, heard it clatter at his feet and vaguely realized it was a miracle he hadn't shot off one or both of his feet. Next step, try for the buckle one more time, with double clumsy sausage fingers that were slick with blood.

From the back, one of his soldiers leaned across Lampone's wounded shoulder, triggering a shotgun blast that made Lampone feel as if a pro-class heavyweight had punched him in the ear. Next thing he knew, the moron jacked the shotgun's slide action and dropped the smoking empty shell into the gap between Lampone's collar and his neck.

"Godda—"

The second blast was even worse. Lampone swore he actually felt his eardrum blow, and in a heartbeat he was stone-deaf on his left side, his own curses sounding muffled.

Turning to reach the stupid shooter with his good hand, maybe rip out his voice box if he had strength enough, Lampone saw a bullet drill his soldier's right eye socket, taking out a fist-size chunk of skull behind the ear.

Lampone whimpered, reaching for the buckle on his safety rig again. But that was fuel he smelled, along with all the blood, gunsmoke and panic in the chopper's passenger compartment.

And a little birdie told him he was too damned late.

THE CHOPPER TOUCHED down, then blew when sparks met pungent fumes from punctured fuel tanks. Bolan ducked behind the SUV as shrapnel in all shapes and sizes filled the air, slashing at roadside trees and boulders, raining around him as he crouched with arms crossed overhead.

Inside the flaming wreck, ammo was cooking off and men were screaming. Seconds later, yet another frag grenade exploded at the heart of the inferno, silencing the agonized voices.

Bolan rose, holding his Uzi ready, just in case one of the hunters suddenly appeared, against all odds, to finish it. That was beyond the realm of plausibility, but Bolan hadn't reached his present age by taking careless risks.

With the clamor of battle echoing inside his head, he missed the scuffling noise as Favor squeezed between the two front seats, then launched himself through Bolan's open door. A startled cry from Herrera brought his head around in time to see their hostage sprinting for the tree line, knees and elbows pumping frantically.

It would've felt so right to shoot him, but preserving Favor was the whole point of the exercise. Even a flesh wound, just to slow him, would greatly amplify the problems that remained to them.

And God knew those were bad enough already.

Bolan ran to catch his fleeing hostage just as Herrera vaulted through the open driver's door and joined in the pursuit. They missed colliding by a foot or so, no time or energy for an apology on either side. They left the SUV behind without a second thought, both well aware that anyone who might've tampered with it was already dead.

Favor was sobbing when they overtook him. Bolan reached out to swat at Favor's head, spoiling his balance, at the same time that

Herrera leaped and tackled him. Favor cried out as he was falling, then his impact with the ground emptied his lungs and left him wheezing.

"No more," he gasped. "Just finish it, for God's sake! Shoot me!"

"You've confused us with your business partners," Bolan answered.

"What the hell's the difference?"

"They want you dead," Bolan reminded him. "We're trying to prevent it."

"Right. So you can put me in a cage somewhere until they find a way to shut me up for good."

"You're going back," Bolan said. "You have one more chance to make things right."

"You think I'm giving back the money?" Favor asked. "Man, you must be loaded."

"I was thinking more about your conscience," Bolan said.

"Are we in church now? When did that happen?" Favor asked.

"Think about it on the road," Bolan said, as the two of them hauled Favor to his feet and escorted him back to the SUV.

A secondary detonation from the chopper's fuel tank lit their way. The SUV was getting toasty, but they still had time to shove Favor in back, take their seats and motor on, with only minor baking damage to the paint. Next to the bullet holes and shrapnel scars, it hardly mattered.

Bolan checked out the dashboard gauges as he drove, accelerating cautiously. He saw no fluctuation in the fuel level or oil pressure, no sudden spike in heat beneath the hood. They seemed to be all right.

At least for now.

But other hunters would be coming soon, and Bolan didn't want to meet them on the open road. Somewhere ahead, they might find refuge with the ghosts of Agua Caliente.

Or they might find death.

In either case, they wouldn't just be targets in a shooting gallery. There'd be a chance to fight, perhaps even survive.

The latter would depend on Grimaldi, assuming he could get to them in time.

12

Grimaldi left the Learjet to its handlers, who seemed competent enough to run the post- and preflight checklists by themselves. He gave a wad of money to the man in charge, in exchange for promises that the plane would be ready for turnaround and takeoff within ninety minutes, someone standing by all night if necessary, until Grimaldi returned.

That was step one.

Step two involved Grimaldi double-timing to the terminal, then slowing to a normal walk so the police on duty wouldn't feel a need to stop him, pat him down, delay him with a thousand pointless questions. He was presently unarmed, had thus far violated no existing law in Costa Rica, but he simply couldn't spare the time for cops-and-robbers games right now.

Not when he knew that lives were riding on the line.

He found the taxi stand out front. One aging couple went ahead of him, and then Grimaldi got the second cab in line. He gave the driver an address and got a curt nod in reply, then settled back amid the smells of sweat and stale tobacco to endure the ride.

His cabbie wasn't one of those who liked to talk, a blessing that left Grimaldi to focus on what lay ahead of him. The chopper should be ready when he reached the charter strip. There'd been no warning on his sat line from the Farm of anything amiss. If something *had* gone wrong, and cops were waiting for him, he would try to bluff it out.

They rolled through crowded streets where no one acknowledged the basic rules of driving. Even pedestrians charged into traffic willy-nilly, as if bent on suicide. Grimaldi hoped his driver wouldn't hit one, simply for the fact that it would mean police and more delays. He checked his watch incessantly, then stopped himself with grim determination when he guessed that they'd completed half their journey.

A moment later, traffic started thinning out again. They were now turning back toward the outskirts, where citizens who mattered— those with money—wouldn't be disturbed by aircraft taking off and landing all night long.

The charter company had no name on its sign, but Grimaldi confirmed the address, paid his cabbie and entered the small lighted office. A youngish woman with startling red hair greeted him, heard his name and became superhelpful.

His chopper was ready, of course. The, um, modifications for which he'd paid extra were hardly routine, but the gear had been tested and deemed fully functional. If he was caught with it by the police, she regretted to say that the company had no idea what he'd done with the aircraft after taking delivery. Any unauthorized modifications were not the charter firm's responsibility.

Grimaldi nodded through it all, signed papers, showed his pilot's license and surprised the redhead with another roll of currency. As he explained, while they were moving toward the helipad, the cash should help restore the whirlybird to its original condition after he was gone, with no one in officialdom the wiser.

That produced a bright smile from the woman, almost making the pilot wish he could spare some time for R and R.

Almost.

The helicopter was a modified Bell OH-58D Kiowa, a standard army scout ship built initially for a two-member crew. At some point in its working life, the one that sat in front of Grimaldi had undergone some custom work, including the addition of a sliding cargo door on its port side. More recently, while he was flying from the States, the cargo bay had gained a winch like those used on rescue choppers for pickups at sea.

The other last-minute addition was in the Kiowa's nose, more of a restoration than an add-on, since the military versions of the whirlybird were often armed. This night, the weapon was a GAU 19/A

Gatling gun, Lockheed Martin's tribarreled model in .50 caliber, with a selectable cyclic fire rate of 1,000 or 2,000 rounds per minute.

Depending on the needs of the moment.

Grimaldi would've liked to test the big gun for himself, but he was short on time and every bullet wasted might be one he needed when he reached his destination.

Agua Caliente, here I come, he thought.

And climbed into the pilot's seat.

Cordillera de Guanacaste

"STILL NOTHING, BOSS. Dead air."

Armand Casale glowered at his man who held the crackling radio, then turned to watch the darkness flowing past their north-bound vehicle. Lazaro's man was driving, four more cars strung out behind them in formation, like a military convoy on the move.

They'd lost the helicopter and the men on board. Casale had to face that fact and get around it, use the troops he still had left to find and crush his prey, before…what?

Would they cross the border into Nicaragua? *Could* they cross it, after he'd prevailed upon Lazaro's man to phone ahead and pull some strings with customs?

Maybe. Maybe not.

Rocco Lampone's final message had been garbled, then cut off. At first, Casale thought his man was calling in with news of victory, Favor and his companions dead. Lampone had blurted something about mopping up, then all Casale heard was some ungodly racket that he couldn't recognize. Maybe a scream mixed in there, with the rest of it, but that was likely his imagination.

Now dead air.

"Maybe he got 'em, boss," the soldier with the radio suggested. "You know, just before—"

Casale's glare cut off the rest of it, but now he had to wonder, was it possible? Would they find Favor and the others dead inside their vehicle a few miles farther down the road? Would it be standing near the burned-out ruin of Lazaro's helicopter, with Casale's men cooked in their seats?

"How much longer, do you think?" Casale asked Lazaro's man.

"Señor?" The driver didn't seem to understand.

"Until we find them," he explained. "I mean, if they went down or had to land?"

The driver shrugged. "Who knows? I heard the same as you, over the radio."

Casale scowled. "It can't be too much farther, right? We know they didn't make it to the border. Rocco would've said something. We'd hear it on the scanner, right?"

"Perhaps," Lazaro's man allowed. "If they were forced down on the highway, we should see them soon. If they were shot down, then…"

"Then what?" Casale was afraid that he already knew the answer, but he had to ask.

"A crash landing, *señor,* may not be on the highway. We are passing now through two national parks, Guanacaste to the east and Santa Rosa to the west. A helicopter crash, even nearby, might not be visible from the highway, especially at night. Of course, if there is fire then—"

"Right," Casale interrupted him. "I get the picture."

And it wasn't looking good.

If Rocco screwed this up, Casale thought, I fucking hope he's dead. I hope it hurt like hell.

They drove another mile in brooding silence, then Casale thought he saw something ahead. A glow of some kind, maybe, if his eyes weren't playing tricks on him.

"What's that up there?" he asked Lazaro's man.

"I've no idea, *señor*. Perhaps a car on fire."

"More like a truck," Casale said, "the size of it."

It clicked then, and Casale snapped, "Speed up, for Christ's sake! Show me what this tub can really do!"

They had been making decent time, Casale's taut nerves notwithstanding, but the driver milked another ten or fifteen miles per hour from their vehicle. Behind them, the remainder of the caravan kept pace.

From two hundred yards away he recognized the outline of the helicopter, sitting like the skeleton of some big, prehistoric bird that had been struck by lightning, scorched down to its very bones. The light he'd seen was dying flames.

As the car rolled to a halt, Casale smelled the scent of roasting flesh.

"Christ, boss," one of his soldiers said. "Is that Rocco in there? And Louie? All the others?"

"Settle down," Casale said. "We'll make this right."

And how in hell to I do that? he asked himself.

"Looks like they landed," said another of his men. "I mean, just sitting there. It isn't like they crashed, you know?"

Casale looked again and saw that it was true. Unless the whirlybird had dropped straight down from heaven, on its landing gear, the pilot had to have set it down on purpose, *then* got blown away.

Which told him...what, exactly?

"Look around for signs that anybody else was here," Casale ordered, talking to them all at once. "If Rocco had the bird set down, he had to have a reason."

Going for the kill?

Casale's men fanned out, and had the answer moments later. "Over here," one of them called. "Looks like we've got some tinted window glass. Car window'd be my guess."

Agua Caliente

"So THIS IS WHAT a ghost town looks like," Favor said. He didn't sound impressed.

And, truth be told, there wasn't much to see in Bolan's high beams as they rolled along a main street overgrown long years ago. Some of the buildings that had lined that street in boomtown days had fallen in upon themselves, while others seemed to be in fairly decent shape.

"We're lucky that there's anything at all," he said.

"Lucky," Favor replied. "That's not the word I had in mind."

"You're breathing," Bolan told him. "If it takes them long enough to find this place, maybe you'll live to see tomorrow."

"In a cage, you mean. Where Tony's boys can shank me, poison me or maybe have some fun and set my ass on fire."

"Wages of sin," Herrera said without bothering to glance at Favor.

"Ah, the Good Book," Favor said, sneering. "My wages were deposited in Switzerland, the Caymans and in Nassau, dearie. But you blew your chance to share them when you made the choice to get me killed."

"Guess we should stop discussing it, in that case," Bolan said, "and think about the best way to defend this place."

"You read my mind," Favor retorted. "When I was a kid, I always wished that I could be with Davy Crockett at the Alamo. Of course, in those days, I thought dying for a cause was noble."

"Some still do," Bolan said, "but it isn't what I had in mind."

He drove a little farther, then picked out a place where he could nose the SUV between two crumbled buildings made of stone. A good-size tree had sprouted through the roof of one abandoned structure, and would shield their vehicle from any airborne eyes. A drive-by would reveal it, but he guessed they could uproot some brush and clot the makeshift alley's mouth sufficiently to hide it from a casual inspection, anyway.

"Okay, unload," he said. He looked at Favor. "I don't have the time or energy to chase you anymore. You try to run again, I'll shoot you in the legs. Hear me?"

"I get it, fearless leader. But to make my childhood fantasy come true, I really need a gun."

"Dream on."

"Maybe a stick, at least? I'll kill the snakes, while you play soldier."

"Snakes?" The worried echo came from Herrera.

"Why, certainly, my dear," Favor replied. "What would this veritable Eden be without its serpents?"

There could be snakes, Bolan thought. Hell, there could be jaguars, after all this time.

"Just watch your step," he told Herrera. "Don't shoot if you can possibly avoid it."

Bolan turned to Favor. "If you want a stick, go find one. But remember what I said, and stay where I can see you. If I have to track you, it's a hunt, and you're the turkey."

Favor bowed theatrically. "Your wish is my command."

"Remind me why we bother with him," Herrera said when Favor had moved off to poke among the nearby ruins, looking for his cudgel.

"It's the job," Bolan replied. "Now, which place do you like?"

"For a vacation? None of them," she answered.

"For the Alamo," he said.

"In that case, I think walls *and* windows would be helpful. Hopefully, a roof or part of one. And no damned snakes."

Bolan examined the nearby building, stopping outside the dark shell of an old two-story structure. Turning to find Gil Favor, Bolan whistled at the swindler, waving him to follow them.

"Come on," he said. "I think I found your Alamo."

THE TALK OF SNAKES disturbed Blanca Herrera at a primal level. She pictured fat vipers slinking through the ghost town's ruins, but her own fear made her feel ridiculous. Less than an hour earlier, she'd been involved in desperate gunplay, fighting for her life amid grenade blasts. She had helped to kill men, and their friends still hunted her.

What were a few small reptiles by comparison?

The building Cooper had selected as their makeshift fortress had a portion of its roof intact, though she could see stars here and there, through gaps between its ancient shingles. Other parts had fallen, taking termite-riddled second-story floorboards with them, and lay crumbled on the ground floor with remains of rotting furniture.

Ceding the upper story to its rustling bats and shadows, they explored the ground floor briefly with a flashlight beam. Herrera immediately noted that the doors were gone from every room. Some long-ago inhabitant had taken time and effort to remove them from their hinges, for some reason she couldn't grasp. Scanning the open rooms, Cooper explained that missing doors would make their last-ditch fight more hazardous, but he still thought the building was their best choice, in the circumstances.

His decision, clearly, was influenced by the sprawl of open waste ground just behind the structure, where no trees encroached on knee-high grass. Despite her lack of personal experience with combat landing zones, she saw that the vacant lot would make a fair impromptu helipad.

Herrera was poking into corners, praying that she wouldn't find a snake coiled up in one of them, when Cooper asked, "What's up?" She turned, confused, and found him listening to someone on his telephone. She supposed that he had turned its ringer off to keep it from betraying them to enemies.

She stood and listened to the brief, one-sided conversation. She waited until he had closed the telephone, returned it to his pocket, then she asked, "Our help?"

"It's on the way," he replied, with the suggestion of a smile.

From the shadows, Favor commented, "You mean that something's actually going right?"

"Looks like it," Bolan said. "He's in the air. We've got about an hour to kill before the pickup."

"A delightful turn of phrase," Favor said, huddled in his corner.

Bolan let it pass and said, "The chopper can set down out back, as planned. We'll have to mark it for the pilot somehow, when we hear him coming."

"Flashlights?" Herrera offered.

"That could do it." Bolan hesitated. "If we're otherwise engaged, he can most likely guide on that."

Meaning gunfire, she understood. Explosions and whatever else came with them. Flames and smoke and death.

"They may not find us," she said.

"May not. You're right. But just in case, let's set up for the party."

Herrera kept an eye on Favor while Matt Cooper opened up the duffel bags and started laying out their weapons. She had not paid much attention when he purchased them, simply aware that he spent a fair amount of cash and filled two heavy bags with killing tools. The Steyr and the Uzi she had recognized, along with extra magazines and hand grenades. There was another rifle, too, dismantled, with a telescopic sight attached.

"Two rifles?"

"This one's for long-distance," Cooper said, as he assembled its components. "Just in case."

"Nothing for me, of course," Favor groused from his corner lair.

"You have your stick," Cooper replied.

"Have you considered comedy if this career falls through?"

"I always try to leave them laughing," Cooper answered. Herrera found no trace of humor in his smile.

"You want the Steyr?" he asked. "You did all right with it before."

"Your choice," she said.

"I'll keep the Uzi and the Dragunov," he stated, reaching out to stroke the second rifle as he spoke its unfamiliar name. "Grenades?"

"I've never used them," Herrera said.

"Best leave that bit to me, then."

"If we need them."

"Right."

"How *could* they find us?" Herrera almost cringed, hearing the note of desperation in her voice.

"I don't know," Cooper said, "but it's their game, their turf. Our job is to be ready, if and when they come."

"WHERE CAN THEY GO, except the border?" Haroun al-Rachid asked.

"Don't ask me," Armand Casale snapped. He spun to face Lazaro's man. "We would've heard by now if they were at the border, right?"

The smuggler paused, considered it, then nodded. "Yes. They should have reached the checkpoint by this time, and we have people there. They would alert us, certainly."

"So, *not* the border," Casale said. He could feel the acid churning in his stomach, eating at him.

"Well, they must have gone somewhere," al-Rachid observed. "The car is gone."

"That's brilliant. Anybody ever tell you you're a genius?" Casale said with a sneer.

Al-Rachid stiffened. "I am simply asking you—"

"Too many questions. Let me think for just a goddamned minute, will you? Perfect!"

They'd learned nothing from the burned-out helicopter, less than nothing from the spot where it was obvious some kind of motor vehicle had parked after absorbing small-arms fire. Whatever damage that vehicle had sustained, it wasn't bad enough to stop the driver from departing. No oil leaks, no coolant on the ground, nothing that would give Casale hope of a convenient breakdown on the shoulder somewhere up ahead.

And still, they'd never reached the border.

The people might hide anywhere, but first they had to leave their car. Hiding a man or woman in the woods was easy. Covering an SUV was something altogether different.

He rounded on Lazaro's man again. "There's someplace they could go," Casale said, "and lay up for the night. A flying saucer didn't pick them up. The car went somewhere."

"*Sí, señor.* Of course."

"So, you're a smuggler, right?" Casale forged ahead. "You and your people know this country. You run shit across the border night and day. Most of the time, you pay someone to look the other way, I understand. But when you can't do that, when you get stuck with some hard-ass who won't play ball, what do you do?"

"Kill him," the smuggler said without a second thought.

"What about the shipment? When you have to lay up waiting, dodge patrols, whatever. Where's the one place on this godforsaken stretch of road where you could hide a vehicle?"

"*Señor—*"

"Come on. You know there's someplace. Spit it out."

"There is a place, perhaps," Lazaro's man replied. "But it has not been used for many years."

"By *you*," Casale said.

"Correct."

"But someone else may know the secret, right? The locals, other smugglers, border agents. Someone."

"Well… There *is* a place."

"Damned right, there is. What do you call it?"

"Agua Caliente. No one lives there, not for many years. It is abandoned."

"Even better," Casale said.

"Do you really think these strangers from America would know of such a place?" al-Rachid demanded.

"What I think," Casale told the Arab, "is that someone on their team was smart enough to hire a local guide, or at the very least to pick somebody's brain for information that would help them in a crunch. This is the crunch, and we'd be stupid not to check it out."

"Please note that I believe it is a waste of time," al-Rachid replied.

"It's noted. You can take your people, get back in your car and go look somewhere else. The rest of us are going to this Agua Caliente." He turned to Lazaro's man. "What's that mean?"

"Hot water."

"Perfect."

Turning from al-Rachid to his own men, Casale told them, "Leave this shit and get back in your cars. We've got someplace to check before this night gets any older."

Lugging guns they'd had no chance to use so far, his soldiers hastened to obey. That left al-Rachid and his four men still standing on the blacktop, glaring at Casale.

"Well?" Casale asked al-Rachid.

"You wish to make us scapegoats," the Arab said.

"Whatever. You can tag along or go play somewhere else. Whatever you decide, I'm telling anyone who needs to hear it that you've been a royal pain in the ass to work with from day one."

Al-Rachid seemed to ignore him, coming back with, "I will not permit you to exclude us from completion of the mission."

"Great. Outstanding," Casale said. "Then why don't you quit your bitching, get back in your goddamned car and follow me?"

Al-Rachid stalled for another moment, then turned stiffly and retreated toward his vehicle, the other Arabs trailing him. Casale watched them go, and knew that from that moment forward he would have to watch his back.

What else is new? he thought, and climbed into his car. Lazaro's driver waited for him, with the engine idling.

"So, let's do it," Casale said. "Show me Agua Caliente, and let's see who winds up getting burned."

13

Cordillera Central

Grimaldi held the converted Kiowa gunship at its maximum cruising speed, clocking 133 miles per hour as he followed Costa Rica's rugged mountainous spine on a northwestern course. He had been in the air for twenty minutes, meaning that he had another 125 miles to cover before he reached the GPS coordinates he'd memorized. Another fifty-seven minutes, if the headwind he'd been fighting didn't slow him too much.

The Stony Man pilot had called ahead to tell Bolan that he was on his way, a little reassurance that would be worth nothing if the enemy showed up in force before he got to Agua Caliente. Even if Grimaldi was on time, or beat his own best estimate somehow, he might arrive too late. The effort wasted.

No. There was always revenge.

If he arrived too late to help, Grimaldi stood a fair chance of catching Bolan's enemies red-handed at the scene. In that case, he would slaughter them without compunction, track them from on high and cut them down. If any managed to escape, Grimaldi vowed that he would learn their names somehow and hunt them on his own time, kill them one by one.

He owed the Executioner that much, at least.

Grimaldi watched his instruments, making minute adjustments as the Kiowa ate up the miles. He knew that there was rugged mountain territory underneath him, ancient trees aimed skyward like a field of pungi stakes waiting to impale him if he lost track of his altitude. Grimaldi wished he could've seen the view by daylight, but he wasn't on a pleasure trip.

His course followed the Pan-American Highway, which was basically invisible unless he spotted headlights on the move, but so far they were few and far between. The GPS would have to guide him into Agua Caliente, and he hoped that Bolan had supplied the right coordinates.

Without proper coordinates, he could spend days searching the mountains, all in vain. Grimaldi could feel in his gut that time was short. One miss at this point, and he might as well concede the game.

Except it wasn't in his nature to admit defeat.

Bolan had gone through hell and out the other side more times than he could count, and Grimaldi had been his wingman on a fair percentage of those escapades, risking his life to see the missions through. He tried to tell himself that this time was routine, but that was bullshit.

There were no routine missions in Bolan's world. No milk runs. No jobs where a soldier could let down his guard without ruing the day.

Grimaldi wasn't summoned unless help was desperately needed, as a last resort.

Hoping for a distraction, Grimaldi went through the GAU's checklist one final time. Its sighting mechanism used a mast-mounted television eye, designed for both normal optical and infrared imaging. The trigger protruded from the chopper's joystick, sensitive enough to respond under four pounds of pressure from the pilot's index finger. Two thousand rounds of ammunition rested in the belly of the beast, a long belt with disintegrating links.

One minute's steady firing would be engaged if he set the cyclic rate on maximum, and Grimaldi knew that he'd have to watch his step there, not go wasting precious rounds when any one of them might make the difference.

No sweat.

He had a surgeon's touch with aircraft and their weapons systems.

"Hang on, Sarge," he whispered to the outer darkness as his death bird steadily devoured the miles. "I'm on my way."

Agua Caliente

IT WAS DEAD QUIET in the ghost town. Mack Bolan maintained that silence as he walked his beat, scouting the dark perimeter of his position. He'd grown weary in the building, straining his senses and waiting for sounds that he might never hear. The walk would do him good, he thought, and help him see if there were any weak links in their hastily contrived defense.

The makeshift fortress they'd constructed wouldn't stand against determined enemies. Grenades or concentrated small-arms fire could knock it down. But it was still the best have available in Agua Caliente.

His fondest hope was that Grimaldi would arrive and carry them away before Romano's soldiers found the long-abandoned town. That would be the ideal solution, but experience had taught him that best-case scenarios were rare enough to qualify as minimiracles in their own right.

Still, miracles did happen.

He heard the vehicles before he saw them, just a glimpse of headlights through the trees before the leader of the team called for a blackout. That was smart, but there was no way he could mute the engines, short of killing them and moving in on foot.

How many vehicles? Bolan couldn't be sure unless he counted them. That meant delaying his alert to Herrera and Favor, since they hadn't come equipped with walkie-talkies, but he had to take the chance. Combat intelligence was critical, often the difference between a stunning victory and sudden death.

But maybe he could have it all.

The vehicles were still at least a hundred yards away, advancing slowly, cautiously. Bolan was only three plots from their stronghold, close enough to warn his two companions of the enemy's approach, then double back and gauge their numbers.

Maybe even give them a surprise.

Moving before the thought had finished forming in his mind, Bolan ran back the way he'd come and reached the dark two-story hulk in seconds flat. He called to Herrera through the nearest empty window, heard her soft response at once and broke the news.

"Don't fire unless I do," he told her. "And only then if you have target confirmation. Don't shoot me by accident."

"Won't you be here?" she asked, a rising note of worry in her tone.

"I want to shake them up a little first," he told her. "See what kind of damage I can do before they get this far."

"By all means, lead them somewhere else," Gil Favor urged, from the shadows. "I only have a stick, you know."

"You want a better weapon," Bolan told his lurking shadow, "take one from Romano's boys."

"Oh, thanks so *bloody* much!"

Bolan left Herrera to control the swindler's whining as he turned and double-timed in the direction of the creeping caravan. He had the Uzi, his Beretta and spare magazines for both, plus two flash-bang grenades clipped to his belt. The stunners wouldn't kill, unless he stuffed one in a mobster's mouth, but even in the open air they could create enough chaos to give Bolan an edge.

And that might be enough.

Bolan stopped short as the first car rolled into clear view. He stepped into the tumbled ruins of an adobe house and flattened himself behind the knee-high remnant of a southern-facing wall. The caravan stopped short, brake lights and shadow shapes betraying four full-size sedans. Doors opened on the first vehicle, prompting muttered curses as the dome light flared, then gunmen started exiting the other cars, as well.

It looked like five men to a car, which wouldn't be the worst odds Bolan had ever faced, nor would they be the best. Each man that he could see was carrying some kind of long gun—shotguns, automatic rifles—and he took for granted that they'd all have sidearms, maybe some packing grenades or other party favors.

Bolan judged the distance, reckoned they were close enough to make it work, and took one of the flash-bangs from his belt. He wished that it had been a frag grenade instead, or even thermite, but he'd work with what he had.

Pulling the safety pin, he let it drop but held the spoon in place. He'd have six seconds after he released, before the charge went off, and maybe ten or fifteen seconds after that before the farthest shooters from the blast could spot him.

Long enough, unless he screwed it up.

Holding his breath, Bolan rose cautiously to push-up height behind the crumbled wall and made his pitch.

"KNOCK OFF THE GODDAMNED noise!" Armand Casale hissed as his assembled troops began to mutter uneasily among themselves. He didn't know who might be listening or watching, and he didn't want to give the bastards any help.

Silence fell over his assembled shooters. At the rear, just coming from their car, al-Rachid and his four Arabs didn't need a loose-lip warning. They were *always* quiet, even when they spoke in Arabic, as if afraid Casale might be eavesdropping and translating their words.

"You see what we got here," he told the troops. "We need to search this place from house to house, at least what's left of them. We'll start at this end of the street, and—"

Something struck the ground off to his left, a heavy thumping sound that made Casale think of falling coconuts. One of his soldiers looked down at his feet and murmured, "What the fu—?"

A blinding flash scalded Casale's eyes, as thunder clapped hard hands over his ears. He staggered, clung to his Kalashnikov by instinct as he lost his balance, dropping to one knee. For something like a heartbeat and a half, Casale thought it was a lightning strike, but then his ringing ears picked out the sound of automatic-weapons fire.

"Get down!" he bawled. "Take cover!"

Wasted breath, since those among his soldiers who could think and move were way ahead of him, already scrambling behind and under cars, while someone on the sidelines sprayed their ranks with a machine gun. Crawling on his belly in a thousand-dollar suit, still nearly blind and deaf, Casale scrambled to save himself.

The first rounds missed him, rattling overhead and punching through the body of his vehicle with sounds like hammer strokes. Some of his men were now returning fire, although he wasn't sure they had a solid target. Two of them, he saw, were stretched out twitching on the ground, not far from where he huddled in the mud and weeds. Casale couldn't tell if they were stunned or dying, and he worried more about the others who were fit to fight.

It was a trap, he realized. But how in hell had anyone known he would find the place, much less—?

Forget that shit, Casale told himself. Get after them!

He struggled to a crouch, still dizzy from the close-range blast, but clinging to his SMG with one hand and the nearby car fender with the other. He could stand, Casale thought, and that meant he could move.

He risked a glance across the black sedan's trunk lid and saw a winking muzzle-flash low down, around knee height, directly obvious. Just one, as far as he could tell, and if they had the prick outnumbered that way, there was no time like the present to attack.

"Get up!" Casale shouted to his men, hearing his own words echo inside his head, as if he were inside a cave. "Get up and rush that bastard!"

He was on the verge of leading, thinking maybe he could pull it off despite the tremor in his legs, when yet another blast slammed him back to the ground. This time, it felt as if someone had punched Casale in his solar plexus, emptying his lungs and robbing him of his ability to breathe.

Won't die like this, he told himself, still barely lucid as he fought for oxygen. I fucking well won't!

If this was it and he was going down, at least he'd face the prick who killed him. Take somebody with him when he went.

Gasping and struggling to control his spastic limbs, Armand Casale first rolled over, then rose to all fours, and finally lurched upright. Turning to face the enemy, he learned to breathe again while checking out the safety on his AK-47.

Using every ounce of strength he had to find his voice, Casale bellowed at his men, "Get up and follow me, goddamn it! Follow me and finish this!"

BLANCA HERRERA FLINCHED at the grenade blast, dropping to a crouch behind the stony windowsill she had chosen as her vantage point. A burst of submachine-gun fire immediately followed, answered by assorted other weapons in the night. She saw some of the muzzle-flashes but resisted the impulse to fire at such long range.

Behind her, to her right, Gil Favor occupied a shadowed corner, clutching the gnarled four-foot tree branch he'd picked up outside. "What's happening, for God's sake?" he demanded.

"Quiet!" she snapped back at him.

"With all that noise? You can't be serious. I—"

She rounded on him, steely-eyed. "I told you to shut up," she hissed. "Don't make me tell you twice."

Favor seemed to consider a retort, then slowly closed his mouth and huddled farther back into his corner, cudgel held across his chest.

Another flash-bang detonated near the access road—Herrera could tell their sound apart from that of frag grenades by now—and then more firing echoed through the forest. It appeared that several enemies, having survived Cooper's initial ambush, were attempting to retaliate. She could have brought them under fire from where she was, using the Steyr AUG, but in the darkness and encroaching chaos, she worried that she might hit Cooper by mistake.

A heartbeat later, as if answering her silent thought, a shadow figure darted into view on the periphery of Herrera's vision. She immediately swung her gun in that direction, index finger tightening around the trigger, and was taking up the slack when Cooper softly called to her, "It's me."

She raised the Steyr's muzzle as he passed before her window, watching while their enemies played out some lethal pantomime downrange, firing at shadows. They were burning ammunition at a frantic pace, which Herrera knew might help her side—or not, if the attackers had a large supply.

"How many?" she asked the Executioner, when he stood beside her. She smelled sweat and gunsmoke on his skin.

"Twenty, for sure," he said. "I saw three drop, but only one of them is definitely out."

So, seventeen or nineteen, she thought. If Cooper did his share, she only had to kill another eight or nine armed strangers, if she wanted to survive.

It crossed her mind to offer them Gil Favor, but she knew the game had gone too far for that. They couldn't buy their way out with a single life. Their enemies would want all three. And they would wish to make the dying as long and slow as possible.

At least she would be spared that horror, Herrera knew, as long as she had one shot left and strength enough to curl her finger through a weapon's trigger guard.

"What now?" she asked Cooper.

"I'm going out again," he said. "You stay with Favor. Deal with anyone who tries to come inside. Let me handle the rest."

"But I can help you!" she protested.

"And you have. You are. Right here, right now."

He turned and left the ruined house before she could think of a reply. One moment, he was standing at her side; the next, the shadows swallowed him.

She faced back toward the enemy, whose random fire had nearly sputtered out. Instead of gunshots now, she heard the crunching, cursing noise of their advance. A gang of city boys, attacking through the unfamiliar woods.

Kneeling, she braced the Steyr's muzzle on the windowsill in front of her and waited for the first target to show himself.

HAROUN AL-RACHID WAS both angry and frightened, a mix of emotions he did not enjoy. The fighting didn't scare him, since he'd pledged to sacrifice his life for Allah as a teenager and knew that Paradise awaited him, but there was something about stalking through the pitch-black forest, knowing that an enemy was out there with him, *stalking* him, that set his teeth on edge.

The man was used to hit-and-run attacks, staged by surprise, at his initiative. While the Israelis twice had tried to kill him, with a rocket and a car bomb, no one in his brief and violent life had ever hunted al-Rachid like an animal.

The way their unseen adversary stalked him now.

Stalked all of them, in fact.

Who were these people who had led al-Rachid and his companions on a bloody chase halfway across the country? What had become of the "simple" assignment to kill one more witness, thus freeing Kasim al-Bari's Sicilian ally from his legal troubles?

Nothing had gone right since they'd arrived in Costa Rica, and al-Rachid blamed most of it on Armand Casale. Granted, *he* had ordered the airliner bombing before he confirmed that their targets were aboard, but what of it? At least al-Rachid's mistake had not killed any of their own men in the process.

Casale.

Rachid saw the Sicilian up ahead, ducking and weaving through the darkness with unsteady strides. It would be easy to kill him, one shot through the back, but no one else was firing at the moment, and he needed cover.

Soon, perhaps.

As far as he could tell, the so-called town consisted of a single unpaved street, no more than three or four blocks long, flanked on both sides by the remains of crumbling shops and houses. Any standing wall or heap of tumbled stones could hide an enemy. As they fanned out and started creeping through the ruins, al-Rachid knew that each step might well be his last.

The next grenade blast, when it came, made him jump and nearly wet himself. He saw the blast flip one of Casale's men head over heels, somersaulting backward and striking the ground in a bone-crunching sprawl.

The blast, in turn, set most of the Sicilians off again, firing their weapons randomly into the darkness. Al-Rachid and his four soldiers stopped where they were, crouching low, blinking the afterimages of the explosion from their eyes. In such confusion, they could easily be shot by their supposed allies.

Or one of their allies could just as easily be shot by them.

Al-Rachid picked out Casale in the line of ducking, weaving figures, watched him fire short bursts into the shadows where no enemy responded. Wasting precious ammunition. Wasting precious time.

So easy, al-Rachid thought again, before remembering that he had to find and kill the witness first, in order to protect al-Bari and the Sword of Allah from whatever Anthony Romano might reveal, if he was held for trial and sought to bargain for his freedom with authorities. Further, the moneyman they had been sent to silence might himself know details of the Sword's transactions with Romano's Family, and that also had to be erased.

The Saudi motioned his soldiers forward, following a relatively safe distance behind Casale's wild Sicilians. There was no point rushing into danger, after all. Casale emphasized that he was in command, so let him take the risks.

While he, al-Rachid, would claim the prize.

Somewhere along the front line of advance, a new weapon cut loose, strafing Casale's men. Al-Rachid missed its muzzle-flash but saw the result as two gunmen fell. He couldn't tell if they were hit or simply taking cover, and he didn't care. Al-Rachid ducked lower, nearly crawling now, his soldiers emulating his every move. They'd trained for such events, at camps in Syria and Lebanon, but he had never actually used those rusty skills.

Now, he thought, they just might save his life.

The front line's brisk advance had slowed, ground almost to a halt, in fact. The Arab terrorists slowed their pace accordingly, determined not to overtake Casale's men. Along the front line, automatic weapons stuttered, pouring fire into the night.

Al-Rachid wished they had tracer ammunition, so at least he could determine where their shots were going, but no one had planned on fighting a pitched battle in the dark. They had to make do with what they had, whether or not the gear was adequate.

One of his men leaned in to whisper in al-Rachid's ear, asking him, "What shall we do?"

"Nothing," al-Rachid softly replied. "We watch. We wait."

BOLAN HAD RIGGED his last flash-bang grenade to serve him as a booby trap, pulling the pin and wedging the bomb between two stones where it seemed likely that advancing enemies would jar it loose. It was a gamble, since they might step around or over it, might advance along a wholly different path, in fact, but it paid off. He was rewarded with a final blast, the image of a rag-doll figure vaulting through the air, and then he let the front line have another taste of Uzi fire.

He saw two shooters drop, uncertain whether they were dead or wounded, then the others all let go at once, scrambling for cover while they sprayed the shadow forms of long-abandoned shops and homes with automatic fire. Bolan heard bullets pinging off the stones around him, staying well below the line of fire for normal ricochets as he fell back.

The leading hunters still had thirty yards or so to crawl before they reached the house where Herrera stood guard. He meant to balk them all the way, take out as many of them as he could, but Bolan knew the lady would be forced to pull her own weight. And Gil Favor's, too.

Bolan found a new vantage point, settled in and watched the skirmish line approach him. They were nervous, rightly so, but drawing courage from the racket that their weapons made. Perhaps they truly thought that pouring countless rounds into the night would guarantee a hit eventually.

Bolan lined up his shot, then rattled off the last rounds from his Uzi's magazine within three-quarters of a second. Ducking to reload, he heard and felt the storm break over him again, but didn't get the sense that any of his enemies were targeting his muzzle-flash specifically.

That told him two things, off the top: his foes weren't trained in guerrilla tactics, and he'd spooked them to the point where they weren't thinking clearly.

Reloaded now, he crept back underneath a hail of bullets, toward the nearest ruin on his right. That put him three houses away from Herrera, and he hoped to stall them there.

Bolan hoped that the woman had enough restraint to keep from firing, even now, with real-life targets close enough for her to drop them with the AUG. If she could just be cool, lie low and wait, they still had hope. But it was ultimately her call, and she had to play the cards as they were dealt.

Secure for the moment at the junction of two crumbling walls, Bolan stopped long enough to catch his breath. Outside, the gunfire rattled, and he heard the hunters scrambling over stony ground, advancing steadily.

A few more yards, he thought. Just come a little closer.

And he'd give them a surprise.

14

Gil Favor knelt in darkness, felt the moisture from fresh grass and lichen soaking through his trousers at the knees but didn't care. Gunfire was hammering and rattling through the ruins that his captors chose to call a village, as if anyone would ever settle there again. The men who sought to kill him were advancing, only yards away now, and he fought the urge to bolt, to blindly flee.

Why not?

Why wait and let them kill him like a rat in a trap?

Because he had nowhere to go, and he was sick of running. Even as a wealthy fugitive, allegedly protected by corrupt police and politicians, he had known that it might come to this. Now, if he fled into the unfamiliar night he would be lost in minutes, stumbling aimlessly about until he met someone who recognized him.

Someone with a gun who'd cut him down.

Better to die fighting, perhaps, and salvage some small vestige of his dignity.

He clutched the sturdy four-foot stick that he had found outside while they were searching for a place to wait and make their final stand. At first, he'd thought it would be rotten through, and he'd been startled to discover that it felt as solid as a custom walking stick, lacking a shiny finish only to complete the transformation.

Never mind.

He wasn't going to a fashion show, but rather to a slaughterhouse. As long as it could bruise flesh and shatter bones, the cudgel would do well enough.

Favor kept both eyes on the woman, crouching at her window with the automatic rifle at her shoulder, tracking targets in the night.

Cooper had warned her not to fire unless the threat was critical and immediate, and Favor wondered if that meant letting the bastards stroll in through the door or drop down through the gaping roof.

Outside, the battle sounded pretty immediate and critical right now, but if the woman's disciplined silence could keep those wolves from their door a bit longer, then more power to her.

For when the shooters found them, she could only stop so many. They would soon be overrun, and she would be killed unless she chose surrender—and they'd kill her even then; who was he kidding? After that…

Distracted as he was, with gunfire ringing in his ears, Favor was barely conscious of the scrabbling sound outside, beyond his chosen corner of the room, until it was repeated twice. A scraping, stealthy sound, as of…footsteps?

He almost called to Herrera, but it seemed more vital that she watch the firefight's progress and be ready when the shooters came against their so-called safehouse. Favor should be competent enough to peer outside and see if someone was approaching from the rear.

All it required was nerve.

He found it, somehow, rose on trembling legs, using the long stick to support him as he found his balance. When he had it, Favor edged in the direction of the back door he had spotted early on, when they first occupied the ruin. Like the front door, it was narrow, built for people who were generally smaller than himself, and it retained no vestige of a working door.

Favor crept toward the aperture and stopped beside it, hunched and listening. He heard the scraping sounds again, most definitely footsteps over stone, but couldn't tell how many prowlers were approaching. Favor reckoned he could take one by surprise, but after that, he was as good as dead.

Get ready!

He edged closer to the rock wall, left shoulder against it as he raised the cudgel. It was longer than a baseball bat, and heavier, but Favor still approximated the familiar stance from schoolyard games, in which he'd hit his share of long fouls and home runs.

Keep your eye on the ball.

A gun's muzzle came through the doorway, sweeping and probing as if sniffing the air for a fresh scent of prey. It hovered for a moment, then edged farther forward, showing him a length of polished barrel with a hand—the left—supporting it.

Still Favor waited, knowing that it wouldn't be enough to strike the weapon down. He had to get the man behind it, or his effort would be wasted, maybe even suicidal.

Seconds seemed to drag like hours, while the sounds of combat neared. At any moment, he expected Herrera to start firing through her window, then he knew the enemy before him would charge through the doorway, spraying bullets.

Just another second now.

Holding his breath, afraid of making any slight sound, Favor was feeling dizzy when the profile of a narrow, ratlike face appeared beyond the doorjamb, peering forward. Favor didn't recognize the man, of course, but knew his type. They were a staple in the world he had deserted when he stole his billions and took flight for parts unknown.

The profile had become a head and shoulders edging forward, still no glance to right or left. A fatal oversight.

When Favor swung, he put his weight and his abiding rage behind it, swinging through the target as he'd always been instructed, first in baseball, then in golf. The club made solid, satisfying contact with his would-be killer's face and dropped the shooter sprawling on his back.

Not good enough, Favor thought.

In the movies, psycho-killers always jumped back up. Moral of the story—if you put them down, you had to *keep* them down.

Checking the doorway quickly, to be sure no other gunmen lurked outside, Favor returned to stand over the fallen gunman, raised his club and brought it slashing down onto the bloodied face. Again. And yet again.

When it was obvious the shooter wasn't going anywhere ever again, Gil Favor dropped his club, retrieved the dead man's rifle—and found Herrera watching from her window lookout post with an inscrutable expression on her face. He couldn't tell if she was worried, angry or resigned.

He closed the gap between them, dropped beside her in the shadows. "I can help," he said. "It's really me they're after anyway."

"All right," she said, after a pause. "You watch the back and stay alert. Don't shoot unless you absolutely have to. And if I start shooting, come to help."

Grinning, Gil Favor ran to take his battle post.

BOLAN SAW SHADOWS closing on him, even though they didn't know what awaited them. None of the advancing shooters had a fix on his location, and they wouldn't unless Bolan fired again, or one of them tripped over him. He could escape now, slip away and put the bloody scene behind him. A coward might have done exactly that.

But Bolan had a job to do, compelled by duty and a sense of honor that forbade him from putting himself before others. He couldn't ditch Herrera, couldn't leave Grimaldi in the lurch, couldn't even let Favor receive what was probably his just due.

Bolan waited, sighting down the barrel of his Uzi toward the nearest of his enemies. He wasn't sure how many still remained, but there were enough to do the job if he made any critical mistakes.

And right now, even a small mistake could be critical.

His nearest mark was twenty yards away. The house where Herrera guarded Favor was some thirty yards behind him. He could stop a few more of the hunters here, with any luck. Maybe divert the rest and buy a bit more time.

Decision made, he stroked the Uzi's trigger, spitting death along the ragged skirmish line of gunmen shambling toward him. Bolan saw one go down, twitching, then the others dropped like dominoes, some of them well before his bullets reached the places where they'd stood.

As gunfire hammered back at him, Bolan knew they were getting used to playing tag for keeps. They dived for cover faster than they had at first, and covered more effectively. Of five or six men visible when he'd begun to fire, this time Bolan was only confident of one hit, maybe two.

It wasn't good enough.

He backpedaled, staying below their line of fire as bullets laced the night above him. None of them were great marksmen, but then again, they didn't need to be. A single lucky shot would put him down as quickly and effectively as any expert sniper's killing round.

Bolan made sure to keep moving away from the ruin where Herrera and Favor were hidden. He triggered a single round from the Uzi to keep the hunters on track, then ducked lower as another storm broke overhead.

Something fell beside him, landing heavily and wobbling as it rolled. Instinctively, he recognized the hand grenade without really seeing it, knew he had seconds to leap for his life.

Bolan leaped, thunder blooming behind him, battering his ears and tossing him through a long, unplanned somersault. He hit the ground rolling, the way he'd been trained, aware of multiple sharp pains that could be gouging stones or shrapnel wounds.

No time to stop to check, since they had definitely spotted him this time. He rolled, found partial cover in the shadow of a collapsed house and brought the Uzi back to target acquisition.

It was time to fight or die.

ARMAND CASALE WHIRLED as someone clutched his sleeve, stopping short as his SMG barrel swung toward the face of Haroun al-Rachid.

"What the hell?" he demanded.

"We're running in circles," the Arab complained. "Chasing who? Where is this Gilbert Favor we've been seeking all along?"

"If I knew where he was, he'd have a bullet in his head," Casale snapped, raising his voice to make it heard over the sounds of gunfire moving steadily away from them. "Listen, we don't have time for a debate right now."

"We should *make* time," al-Rachid insisted, clinging to the Sicilian's arm.

"First thing you need to do," Casale warned him, "is let go of me and take a long step back. Okay?"

The Arab blinked at him, then almost grudgingly released his sleeve. The backward step was not forthcoming.

"Now," Casale said, "unless you've been asleep the past few

hours, you'll remember that we tracked Favor to this shit hole. We're looking for him, but we have to take care of his people first. Get it?"

"I'm not an idiot," al-Rachid informed him.

"Great. Stop acting like one, then, why don't you?"

Glowering, al-Rachid said something in Arabic and made a show of spitting on the ground between them, near Casale's shoes. Casale stared at him, putting the full weight of his malice in the look.

"You talk about us wasting time," he told al-Rachid, "but you think standing here and jawing in the middle of a firefight is a bright idea? If you've got something else to say, speak English. Otherwise, step off!"

The Arab's next move was meant to be a sucker punch, but he was too angry to diguise his body language. Casale saw the Arab's weapon swinging up and toward his face, raised his own SMG to block it, and the two guns came together with a solid clack. Casale followed through, aiming his free arm's elbow at the Arab's snarling face, but al-Rachid was quicker, raising his own empty hand to fend off the blow.

Casale lost it, slashing a kick at al-Rachid's lower body, grunting as his heel missed the family jewels and pummeled a thigh. Al-Rachid barked something else in Arabic and swung his rifle toward Casale's head again. The mobster raised his SMG to block the swing and cursed as the AK's stock hit his knuckles.

Dropping his weapon from numb fingers, Casale saw al-Rachid step backward, clearly preparing to level his weapon and fire. It was do-or-die time, and Casale reacted on sheer killer instinct, lunging forward instead of recoiling, grabbing the Kalashnikov with both hands while he slammed his forehead squarely into al-Rachid's face.

They fell together, arms and legs entangled, gouging and punching with the AK-47 pinned between them. Casale wondered why al-Rachid's men hadn't joined the fracas, then he had no further time for thought. Fingers were clutching at his throat, squeezing, and tiny colored lights were flashing on the insides of his eyelids.

Wedged against al-Rachid as they lay grappling on the ground, Casale couldn't reach the pistol holstered in his left armpit. Instead, he groped under his ruined jacket for the sheath that held his WASP injector knife, drew it and found the trigger button with his thumb.

Al-Rachid had actually rolled Casale onto his back, was riding him and gouging at his Adam's apple with determined thumbs, when Casale drove the 5.5-inch blade between his ribs. He pressed the trigger, wasting no time, and enjoyed the look on the Arab's face as his abdomen filled with a bubble of CO_2 gas chilled to minus sixty degrees Fahrenheit.

Casale didn't know how long the gas would take to kill al-Rachid, and he was past the point of taking chances. With a final mighty heave, he gave the blade a twist and dragged it forward, scraping hard along one of the dying Arab's ribs. Blood jetted from the wound, drenching his shirt and jacket. Some of it was warm, the rest as cold as beer straight from the tap.

Casale rolled, taking al-Rachid to his left and squirming free of the Arab's death grip. Rising, he watched his victim shiver through the final spasm of his death throes, heels drumming the ground.

"Chill out," Casale said, and snickered to himself.

He reached down to retrieve his submachine gun, turned back toward the sound of gunfire fading in the middle distance—and found al-Rachid's four shooters staring at him over gun sights.

Casale reckoned this was bad, but weariness and his instinctive temperament refused to let him grovel.

"What?" he challenged them. "Your homeboy lost it. What's the beef? *I* run this show, goddamn it! Understand? If you don't like it, you can—"

A word from one of them, dead center in the line, and then all four were hosing him with bullets, the combined impact of their full-auto fire lifting Armand Casale off his feet and flinging him away.

CROUCHED IN THE DARKNESS, Blanca Herrera watched the skirmish line of gunmen racing off away from her position, following Matt Cooper's train into the night and firing as they ran. She said a swift and silent prayer for the American, then concentrated on her own plight and Gil Favor's.

For they still were not alone.

Cooper had drawn off some of those who sought to kill them, but others still advanced toward their hideaway. Herrera could hear them moving closer by the minute. At the back door, Favor waited with the rifle he had seized from his fallen enemy, alert to any danger from that quarter.

Herrera didn't know if she could use an automatic rifle, much less hit a moving human target with it, but she needed help. One gunman had already found their hideaway, and others were close by.

A shadow loomed in front of Herrera's window, blotting out the faint starlight beyond. She bit her lip to keep from gasping, knew the shooter couldn't see inside her pitch-black cave from where he stood, unless he used—

The flashlight's beam lanced past her, playing over lichen-covered stone. Instead of waiting for the light to find her, Herrera took the shot, aiming as she'd been trained for the target's center of mass. One shot from less than twenty feet away, and if her target wasn't dead before he hit the ground, he would bleed out in minutes flat.

Before the echoes of her single shot had died away, all hell broke loose. Multiple weapons began pouring fire through the windows of Herrera's retreat, their bullets ricocheting off the stone walls and whining like a cloud of deadly insects.

She ducked and crawled below the storm, saw Favor doing likewise at his backdoor post. At last she rolled behind a broken-down interior wall, safe from direct frontal fire for the moment, still painfully vulnerable to ricochets from behind.

A sudden burst of gunfire from the back door snapped her head around in that direction, just in time to see Gil Favor squeezing off another burst. He ducked back as a swarm of bullets answered him, their one path of retreat cut off.

And when he met her gaze, the swindler smiled.

Somehow it gave her new hope. Not of escape, which seemed impossible, or even of survival, which appeared increasingly unlikely.

No.

. She simply hoped to make a decent fight of it and give the bastards something to remember as they stood over her corpse.

Two figures rushed the doorway facing Agua Caliente's over-grown front street. Herrera rose from her crouch and stitched them with a chest-high burst from left to right, dropping one man facedown, pitching the other backward through the open portal. When the autoweapons blazed again outside, she reckoned there were two fewer guns.

But still enough to do the job.

Not yet, she told herself. They'll have to work for it.

More fire rattled from Favor's AK-47, and he seemed to be holding the fort all right against however many shooters sought to overrun his post. Herrera could offer him no help, nor he to her, but they were still a team.

That made her laugh, and she was still laughing when a grenade arced through the window she had lately vacated, bounced once and wobbled toward the wall that shielded her. She ducked back under cover, clapped both hands over her ears and hoped she would survive the thunderclap to slay a few more of her enemies.

GRIMALDI WOULD'VE SEEN the massacre in progress from his cockpit, tracking muzzle-flashes and explosions flaring on the darkened landscape down below, even without the GPS and other instruments to confirm his positions.

This was the place, all right. No doubt about it. But he couldn't pick out Bolan or his comrades from the chopper's present altitude—and likely not at all, by sight, unless he set down in the middle of the maelstrom.

If naked eyes and instruments were lacking, he still had his wits and long combat experience to help with target acquisition. One low-flying circuit of the killing ground should tell him what he had to know, with any luck at all.

Grimaldi started with the proposition that his friends would be out-numbered, maybe cornered by their enemies. That set his eyes and mind to work searching for patterns in the muzzle-flashes, the explosions, and the answers came to him with no great difficulty after all.

The chopper's spotlight helped.

Below him, more or less dead center in the midst of the chaotic action, shooters had surrounded what appeared to be a crumbling edifice of stone, pouring their fire into its doors and windows, while a lonely pair of weapons stuttered in response. And farther out, moving in a northwesterly direction, half a dozen shooters tracked a lone quarry who paused from time to time, returning fire.

Troop disposition told a story, and the numbers didn't lie.

Grimaldi nosed his gunship over, swooping first against the shooters who were harrying their quarry through the woods. He came at them from the southeast, skimming along their skirmish line and triggering a long burst from the .50-caliber GAU 19/A as he swept past.

Thirty-three armor-piercing rounds per second raked the men he'd never met, whom he would never see alive, up close and personal. The spotlight showed Grimaldi all he had to know. He understood the kind of hell he had unleashed on them and wished them speedy deaths, hoping he wouldn't have to make a second pass.

He banked the Kiowa, dropped under treetop level as he followed Agua Caliente's narrow main street toward the other site of homicide in progress. Gunmen clustered at the southeast corner of a tumbledown stronghold, distracted from their penetration by Grimaldi's strafing run against their friends.

Several gunners started firing at him as he neared them, but Grimaldi froze them in his spotlight's beam, then hosed them with a stream of bullets weighing 759 grams each, ripping through flesh and bone at 2,800 feet per second. Most of the hunters went down in a heap; a couple of them dodged to save themselves, running around behind the house they had been trying to invade.

Grimaldi looped around to follow them, caught them as they joined forces with a smaller team back there. His spotlight was pinned on their startled, frightened faces, but he had no time to wonder what was going on inside their heads. Another trigger stroke, another humming burst from the Kiowa's prow and everything inside those heads was suddenly outside, a crimson spray painting the structure's stony wall.

Grimaldi took the chopper higher, played his light over the cut-rate Alamo and saw two figures staring up at him, arms raised to shield their eyes. One was a woman, very obviously. Both were packing automatic rifles, but they made no move to aim and fire at him.

So far, so good.

But neither one was Bolan.

After checking out the crumbling fort's perimeter for any sign of hostile movement, Grimaldi turned once more toward the scene of his first pass against the hostiles. Movement on his left, a rush of pint-size shadows, drew Grimaldi's eyes and he saw four men running hell-bent toward where their cars were parked, all in a tidy row.

He swung around to track them, knowing their escape could only mean more trouble somewhere down the line. Grimaldi took no pleasure from the mopping up, but it was still a job requiring his most diligent attention.

On the ground, his quarry heard him coming, turning as a single man to face the Kiowa, even before his spotlight locked on target, pinning the quartet at center stage. Their muzzle-flashes winked at him before Grimaldi pressed his trigger and cut loose with the Gatling gun.

One second, four men stood before him, angry and defiant, automatic weapons blazing. And the next, Grimaldi watched them come apart, ripped into bloody tatters and discarded by the stream of death that passed around and through them, sweeping on until his finger lifted from the trigger and it ended. Finally.

Stone-faced in the light from his instrument panel, Grimaldi put the Kiowa through one more turn and started looking for a place to set it down.

BOLAN PASSED by the idling helicopter with a hand raised, greetings and a time-out signal all in one, as he backtracked in search of Herrera and Favor. They were just emerging from the stone house as he got there, both with rifles in their hands. He recognized the Steyr AUG, but frowned at the Kalashnikov in Favor's hands.

"You won't need that," he told the fugitive.

"It's empty, anyway," Favor said. "But it came in handy for a while." He tossed the weapon backward through the open doorway, where it clattered on impact with the ground.

"You're both all right?" Bolan asked.

"Fine," Herrera said.

"I'm tired of bloody Costa Rica," Favor added.

"Just as well," Bolan replied. "We're leaving."

"What, in that?" Favor asked.

"Yeah. To San José. We'll see what's waiting for us there."

"Maybe I ought to keep the rifle, after all."

"You're covered," Bolan said. "Let's go."

Grimaldi took the chopper up when they were strapped into their seats, Bolan in the copilot's place, Herrera and Favor in the rear.

"You made good time," Bolan said as they left the killing ground behind them, heading southward.

"It looked a little close. Who were those guys?" Grimaldi asked.

"Tony Romano's people, I suppose," Bolan replied.

"Are you expecting more of them before we split?"

"It's hard to say. We'll keep the hardware handy while we can. Cover our bets."

"And when we get back to the States?" Grimaldi asked.

"The Feds take over, more or less."

"Meaning?"

"I'm not sure yet."

But Bolan was already thinking past their flight from San José to the United States. He had unfinished business with the men who'd tried to kill him here.

And he had never liked loose ends.

Epilogue

New York City

The high-rise stood a block off Broadway, near Trinity Church. Once upon a time, its penthouse occupants could have gazed from their tinted windows upon the World Trade Center.

No more.

New York had changed in fundamental ways that went beyond the alteration in its skyline. Promoters would insist that the city still had its old panache, that it was battered but unbowed.

And yet...

There were men at large, some known by name, who thought of 9/11 as a firecracker and longed to play with dynamite, instead. They wanted higher body counts, more carnage in the streets, a wave of shock and awe that would inflict, at last, a mortal wound upon American society.

He knew the enemy this time, had traced them with some timely aid from Hal Brognola and the techs at Stony Man.

And he was there to pay a visit, in his status as the Executioner.

Upon Bolan's arrival in the Empire State, a flying squad of Feds had claimed Gil Favor, whisked him off to some presumably secure facility, from which he would emerge to testify against Antonio Romano in due course. However, covert intelligence had told Bolan that Romano hadn't severed his connection to the Sword of Allah. That, in fact, he would be meeting with a leader of that group, this very day.

Tony Romano had done piecework for the Sword, and he could almost certainly identify some of its ranking covert agents in the States. Whether they were sleepers living off the grid, or terrorists disguised as diplomats, Romano could expose them if he chose to do so, in a bid for mercy from the courts.

Given the history of Mob informers during recent years, Bolan suspected that Sword of Allah's strategists had little faith in Romano or his sacred oath of *omertá*.

They might decide to kill him, which was fine with Bolan, but he worried more about the terrorists themselves than any mobster in Manhattan. When the choice came down to loan sharks versus the Apocalypse, it wasn't even close.

He had a pass card for the underground garage, and his Lexus—confiscated from a smuggler in Miami—and his thousand-dollar suit added a solid touch of reassurance for the rent-a-cop on duty at the gate. The guard made no attempt to check his driver's license, much less search the vehicle for weapons.

He was in.

Now, all he had to do was stay alive.

"YOU'RE BLAMING *ME* for all this fucking heat? It wasn't my boys who went off and bombed a fucking plane with a couple hundred people on board."

Tony Romano understood his guest's aversion to profanity, regarded it as hypocritical in one so bloody-handed and so took every opportunity available to salt his conversation with obscenities. It might be childish, but at least he got to watch the bastard squirm.

"The fact remains," Kasim al-Bari argued, "that you are the one facing trial for your life. It is your link to the Sword, not mine, that draws this 'heat,' as you describe it, from the government and media alike."

"What dream world are you living in?" Romano asked, remembering too late that he had failed to drop another F-bomb. He stalked across the wide room to his massive picture window. "Take a look, will you? There used to be a couple towers standing over there, in case you never heard about it. People don't forget that shit around New York, the way they do in Baghdad."

"I am not Iraqi," al-Bari said stiffly.

"Like I give a shit," Romano said with a sneer. "You came to me, as I recall, because you couldn't get the cash you needed from a goddamned ATM, and Sachs Fifth Avenue was all sold out of high-tech military shit. You rang me up because your Russian buddies left you high and dry."

"I hate the Russians."

"And, apparently, you hate me now. Looks like you're running out of fucking comrades, Comrade."

"I feel nothing for you," al-Bari told him, deadpan. "What I *need* from you is some assurance that you will remain discreet concerning our…arrangements."

"Listen up," Romano said. "I'm not a fucking rat, okay? This ain't Sammy Gravano you've been dealing with. I've never told the cops a goddamned thing about my business, and I never will."

Al-Bari offered him a narrow smile. "With all respect," he said, "it's not *your* business that concerns me."

"You aren't thinking straight," Romano said. "You sit here in my living room, accusing me of rolling over on you? If that's what I wanted, don't you think this meet would be a setup? Did you smell Homeland Security when you were on your way up in the elevator? Maybe you should check that couch you're sitting on, see if I've got a G-man hidden underneath it."

"There are devices," al-Bari said.

"Devices, huh? You've got three men out in the waiting room. Which one carries your sweeper for you?"

"Sweeper?"

"Don't play dumb. The bug detector. Which one has it?"

"I believe, Mohammed."

"Right. So drag his ass in here and have him sweep the place. I give you leave."

Al-Bari shrugged. "It might prove nothing."

"So, I've got devices, but I don't. Is this the kind of bullshit double-talk you fringe types go for over there?"

"Insults are not productive, yes?"

"That's funny. You come into my house, calling me a rat, but insults turn you off. Go figure, huh?"

"I have expressed concern," al-Bari said, correcting him.

"Your…brotherhood…was once well-known for keeping secrets, but no more."

"Some of us hold the line," Romano answered, fuming. "And I'm one of them."

"Much better for us all, I think, if you had managed to eliminate this final witness."

"Do we need to talk about the fucking plane again? I'm sick and tired of going around in circles on this thing. What's done is done."

"But my work is not done," al-Bari said. "I still have much to do."

"You'll have to do it on your own, or find somebody else to help you out," Romano answered. "I'm under a goddamned microscope, as you already pointed out."

"But you have friends. Contacts."

"I might," Romano answered cautiously. "It all depends on what you've got in mind."

BOLAN RODE THE ELEVATOR from the basement to the twenty-second floor, then shifted to the service stairs. He didn't have a copy of the key required to reach the penthouse level via elevator, and didn't care to risk a premature encounter with Romano's bodyguards in circumstances where he'd have no combat stretch. The staircase wasn't great, but it was better than a six-by-eight-foot metal coffin, dangling on steel cables over an abyss.

On twenty-four, he paused and drew the sleek Beretta 93-R autoloader from its shoulder rig, the sound suppressor attached. With gun in hand, he climbed the last four flights to reach the penthouse level of the high-rise. Romano had the floor all to himself—which did not mean he lived there alone. Mafia dons *always* had guards around them, and there might be servants of the noncombatant kind, as well. Bolan would have to watch for those, and spare them if they made no hostile moves against him.

On twenty-four he tried the door handle—no keyhole showing on his side, no peephole window in the metal door—and was relieved to feel it turn. Holding his breath, he eased it open half an inch, peered through the crack and saw no one. Next, listening, he stood and waited without breathing until someone coughed, nearly a minute later.

Bolan estimated that the sound had come from fifty feet away and to his right. Because the service stairs were situated in the far southeastern corner of the building, that made perfect sense. It also told him that he could emerge and make his cautious way to find the enemy without immediately being seen.

Unless they had surveillance cameras pointed at the stairwell door, of course. Or someone sitting in the corner that he couldn't see from where he stood, prepared to counter stealth attacks.

It was a risk he had to take, unless he meant to turn around and leave without accomplishing his goal. Since that thought never crossed his mind, Bolan pushed forward, leading with his pistol, checking first behind the open door, then high along the wall for cameras.

Nothing.

Another cough came from his right, beyond a corner, then resolved itself into a pair of voices. Both were male, and while he couldn't make out any of their words yet, Bolan recognized the sound of small talk when he heard it. They were killing time, two guys at least, and maybe more. The very fact that they were idling on the penthouse floor told Bolan they had to be Romano's bodyguards.

Once Bolan stepped around the corner and revealed himself, he'd be committed to whatever happened next. If there were six or seven guns, instead of two, he might be fatally surprised. But turning back had never really been an option.

Bolan eased into the open, pistol steadied in a firm two-handed grip and seeking target acquisition. He saw two men of average height, standing a trifle closer than his ears had led him to believe. They were engaged in conversation, one with his back turned, the other's face obscured by his companion's head.

Bolan advanced. One step, another and a third. Closing the gap. At twenty feet, he put a 3-round burst between one shooter's ears, slamming the guy face-forward into his companion with a splash of crimson as the only warning. Both of them went down, but Bolan couldn't tell at first if he had dropped the second man for good or merely stunned him.

That was answered when the soldier on the bottom started cursing through a bloody mask, shoving his late friend to the side and groping for a weapon underneath his sport coat. Bolan fired a 3-round burst into his slick red face and ended it.

Who else?

It seemed unlikely that Romano would have only two men watching him, but there were likely more inside the penthouse proper. Then again, Bolan supposed, since Romano was being shadowed by the Feds, intent on making sure he didn't miss his next court date, maybe the Don had begun to think that he was safe.

Which only went to show how wrong a guy could be.

"DID YOU HEAR something?"

Interrupted in the middle of a thought, Kasim al-Bari hesitated for a moment, listening, then shook his head. "Nothing. Now, as I—"

"There was something," Romano insisted, brushing past him, moving toward the nearest doorway.

Romano reached the door and opened it. "Hey, Jimmy!" he called out. "Rico!"

Al-Bari stood and waited, watching as Romano's men appeared, listened to orders issued in a voice low-pitched to ward off eavesdropping, then hastened to obey.

"Could be a false alarm," Romano said as he returned, passed by al-Bari once again and walked directly to a redwood cabinet mounted on the study's western wall. "But, what the hell. Can't be too careful, right?"

Before al-Bari could respond, Romano had the cabinet open. Racked inside it were three shotguns, two rifles and several handguns. "Party favor?" he inquired, half smiling.

"Are we in some danger?" al-Bari asked.

"I should have the answer to that question in—"

A gunshot echoed through the penthouse, followed swiftly by two more in rapid-fire, with angry voices shouting.

"Okay," Romano said. "Take that as a yes."

The mafioso chose a pistol, checked its load and stuck the gun inside his waistband. Next he took a shotgun from the rack of upright weapons, pumped its slide and started rooting in a drawer for extra cartridges.

"Last chance," he said.

Al-Bari started forward, then stopped short, hands rising slowly as his host pointed the shotgun at his face.

"On second thought," Romano said, "maybe that isn't such a hot idea. I mean, for all I know, this could be your setup."

"What are you saying?"

"Bottom line? That I don't trust you any further than I can throw…well, some really heavy shit, okay? You start with insults, now I've got a firefight. Add it up, dipshit."

"You think I would attack your home while I am in it? Allah help me. You are even less intelligent than I supposed."

"Oh, yeah? Let's find out if I'm smart enough to dust your ass. How's that sound to you?"

"Like a foolish plan," al-Bari said, and swallowed hard. He knew that he was balanced on a razor's edge. The next few seconds might decide whether he died this night or lived to see another dawn.

"Wrong answer," Romano said, as he raised the shotgun to his shoulder.

"Wait!" The Arab held both hands in front of him, as if his naked palms could stop a point-blank shotgun blast.

"What for?" Romano asked.

More gunfire crackled from the rooms beyond Romano's private den. Al-Bari heard a man's voice, crying out in mortal pain.

"Whatever you may think," he told Romano, "this is not my doing. I am innocent."

"And I'm your fairy godmother," Romano said. "Nobody's innocent."

"Of this, I mean!"

"Bullshit!" Romano spit. "You think I'm gonna blow the whistle on your little gang of camel jockeys, so you want to take me out. Well, it's been tried before, okay? You blew it, like the rest."

"At least find out if you're correct!" al-Bari said, hating the note of panic in his voice. If he survived this, he would be avenged on the Sicilian for exposing such a weakness in himself.

"Oh, sure. You want to stroll out there and have a word with your *amici?* Make believe you've got nothing to do with it?" Romano paused, seemed to consider his own words, then said, "All right. Why not?"

As the Sicilian stepped aside, waggling his shotgun's muzzle toward the door, al-Bari understood his meaning. "You would go out there?" he asked Romano.

"After you," the mafioso answered, smiling.

"But—"

"Move it or lose it, pal. My finger's getting itchy."

So, al-Bari stepped cautiously across the threshold, glancing left and right in search of enemies. The gunfight, from its sound, was still removed from their immediate location by a room or two. The spacious penthouse could conceal him yet, but first—

"Go on!" Romano snarled, prodding al-Bari with his shotgun. Slowly, dragging his feet, al-Bari moved in the direction of the battle sounds, clenching his muscles for the move that would decide his fate.

"I said, go on, damn it!"

When the next shove came, al-Bari pivoted on his left heel, battered Romano's gun aside with his left elbow, lunging for the mobster's face and throat with clawed fingers. Romano struck back, hammering al-Bari's ribs with the shotgun's stock before the Arab's momentum carried them both to the floor.

BOLAN HAD LEFT the first two sentries sprawled in blood, staining the foyer of what appeared to be Tony Romano's front door. He still hadn't seen any closed-circuit cameras, but guessed that someone would discover his intrusion soon. If nothing else, when he went through the entrance to Romano's suite of rooms—assuming that it wasn't locked—there would be no concealing him.

And that was fine.

He neared the door, stretched out his left hand toward the knob, noting that this door had a peephole, pale light visible beyond the fish-eye lens. Before his fingers closed around the knob, a shadow fell across that tiny eye of light, and then the door swung open to reveal a tall man dressed in slacks and shirtsleeves, with his shoulder holster clearly visible.

The shooter gaped at Bolan, made a little squawking noise and started reaching for his pistol. All too late. A Parabellum mangler drilled his forehead and snapped his head back, dropping him across the threshold like some kind of grisly welcome mat.

Behind him, shooter number four was shouting an alarm, recoiling from the body that had tumbled at his feet. In motion, ducking, dodging, he was quicker on the draw than his companion, but it didn't help. Bolan's next round punched through a shoulder, spinning him, blood spurting from the wound.

Still, he was strong, this fourth defender of his master's realm. He took the hit and turned it into something he could use, flinging himself out of the spin and through a leap that lofted him over a nearby sofa, dropping out of sight from Bolan's vantage point in the doorway.

Huddled there, no doubt in grievous pain, the shooter called out to the suite at large, "Incoming! Everybody up and at it!"

Bolan didn't know who *everybody* was, or how many there were, but he could only deal with one foe at a time. Crab-walking toward the couch, he had his 93-R ready when the wounded gunner showed himself, emerging from the other end with his sidearm out and blazing.

Bolan hit him with a 3-round burst, but his target still kept firing as he fell, reflexes taking over, as a dying snake may sink its fangs into the predator that's killed it. Thankful that Romano had no upstairs neighbors, Bolan left the dead man twitching where he lay and moved on, hunting through the richly furnished rooms.

He soon met the two last shooters, who, he guessed, had been sacked out at rest in different bedrooms. Doors came open on his left and right in unison, as if rehearsed or signaled from somewhere behind the scenes. The shooter on his left cut loose immediately with some kind of compact SMG that sounded like a buzz saw, bullets chewing through Romano's furniture and artwork with abandon. On his right, a shotgun hammered twice, filling the air with double-aught buckshot.

Bolan was on the floor by that time, rolling, seeking cover. The shotgunner rushed him, reckless, giving the Executioner time to squeeze his trigger twice and stitch the shooter's abdomen with half a dozen rounds. Their impact stopped him dead and put him down without a whimper, triggering a final blast into the high back of plush recliner.

Bolan's Beretta had no more than four rounds left in its extended magazine. He used three of them, teaching his surviving enemy to keep his head down, then replaced the mag as he was crawling from the sofa to the cover of a tall grandfather clock.

Thus situated, Bolan risked a glance and nearly lost a portion of his scalp to whistling rounds, but the brief look had shown him what he had to know. The angle wasn't perfect, but he had made do with worse in killing situations, and his time was running short.

It wasn't flash-bangs, this time, but an honest frag grenade that Bolan unclipped from his belt. Yanking the pin, he ducked and rolled, drawing the shooter's fire, then pitched a strike from twenty feet.

The target saw it coming, made his choice in nothing flat and charged out of the bedroom, firing as he came. Bolan was waiting for him with the 93-R, hit him with a burst dead center in the chest that blew him back across the threshold, just as the grenade exploded, swallowing his airborne body in a swirl of smoke and flame.

It took a moment for his ears to stabilize, then Bolan heard someone addressing him. The voice came from a point midway between the rooms where he had just killed strangers, calling out, "You want to talk about this shit, or do we do it the hard way?"

"Romano?" he replied.

"Who else were you expecting?"

"We can do this face-to-face," Bolan replied, "or I can blast you out."

"Think twice about that," came the answer. "Anything you throw at me goes through your boss to reach me."

Boss?

Bolan could hear the numbers running in his head, but still he played along. "Okay, I'm listening."

"It's simple. If you want him in one piece, I get a pass. That's it."

"I need to see him," Bolan answered, shifting to a better vantage point after he spoke.

"No sweat. He's got a few lumps on him, thanks to being stupid, but it could be worse. I guarantee it."

Bolan saw Romano just emerging from what had to be the master bedroom, shuffling along behind a human shield. The man he held in front of him was bearded, showing bruises on the right side of his face, the fury in his eyes untempered by defeat. Romano had a pistol jammed against his captive's head, behind one ear.

And Bolan knew that face, from mug shots he had seen at Stony Man.

Your boss.

Romano had his enemies mixed up, prompting a gamble that could only fail.

"All right, you see him," the mafioso said. "Do we have a deal, or what?"

"So, where's my boss?" Bolan asked, rising with the 93-R leveled in a steady two-handed grip.

"Don't shit a shitter, man. I— Hey," Romano suddenly demanded, "who the fuck are you?"

"Call me a bill collector," Bolan said. "Your tab's way overdue."

"You're not… I mean… You want this guy or not?"

"I'll take him off your hands," Bolan said, "but he isn't worth your life."

"Take this, then!" Romano said, putting all his strength into a shove that set Kasim al-Bari staggering forward, while Romano's pistol wavered into target acquisition.

Bolan and the mobster fired together, drilling al-Bari front and back. The Arab grimaced, then his knees buckled and dropped him to the floor. Bolan squeezed the Beretta's trigger three more times in rapid-fire, nine rounds tearing through Tony Romano's chest and face from twenty feet. The mobster went down, twitching, pistol spinning from his lifeless fingers.

Bolan waited for another second, heard a fire alarm begin to clamor somewhere in the high-rise, then retraced his steps in the direction of the service stairs.

No elevator this time, going down, but he had energy to burn. He would be out and gone before police or firefighters arrived. They could sort out the details for themselves, while he reported back to Stony Man.

He wondered, briefly, what would happen to Gil Favor, now that he was not required to testify. Bolan decided that it hardly mattered, either way. The swindler was an outlaw who would likely never learn his lesson, but in the bigger picture he had been a guppy swimming with the sharks.

Bolan knew from hard experience that it wouldn't be long before one of those sharks provoked another deadly encounter.

ROOM 59

THE HARDEST CHOICES
ARE THE MOST PERSONAL....

New recruit Jason Siku is ex-CIA, a cold, calculating
agent with black ops skills and a brilliant mind—a
loner perfect for deep espionage work. Using his Inuit
heritage and a search for his lost family as cover, he
tracks intelligence reports of a new Russian Oscar-class
submarine capable of reigniting the Cold War. But when
Jason discovers weapons smugglers and an idealistic yet
dangerous brother he never knew existed, his mission
and a secret hope collide with deadly consequences.

Look for

THE ties THAT BIND

by

cliff RYDER

**GOLD
EAGLE**®

*Available October 2008
wherever books are sold.*

JAMES AXLER
DEATH LANDS

Thunder Road

Fight or die in the raw and deadly frontier of tomorrow...

Thunder Rider is a self-styled superhero, prowling the Deathlands and serving up mass murder in a haze of napalm and nerve gas. Ryan Cawdor accepts a bounty from a ravaged ville to eliminate this crazed vigilante. But this twisted coldheart has designs on a new sidekick, Krysty Wroth, and her abduction harnesses the unforgiving fury of Ryan and his warrior companions. At his secret fortress, Thunder Rider waits—armed with enough ordnance to give his madness free rein....

In the Deathlands, justice is in the eyes of those who seek it...

Available September wherever you buy books.

THE GOLDEN ELEPHANT

by AleX Archer

**Golden elephants. Tomb robbers. Murder.
Just another day at the office.**

Offered a reward for a priceless golden elephant,
Annja heads to the mountainous jungles
of Southeast Asia. To
pinpoint the artifact's
location, she must meet
with various scholars—
but each expert turns
up dead! Annja fears
someone else is after
the elephant—and her!

In a remote Asian village
lies a priceless artifact—
and a death trap

**Available September
wherever you
buy books.**